T0009297

More Days at the
Morisaki Bookshop

Also by Satoshi Yagisawa

Days at the Morisaki Bookshop

More Days at the
Morisaki Bookshop

A Novel

Satoshi Yagisawa

Translated from the Japanese by Eric Ozawa

HARPER PERENNIAL

NEW YORK • LONDON • TORONTO • SYDNEY • NEW DELHI • AUCKLAND

This is a work of fiction. Names, characters, places, and incidents are products of the author's imagination or are used fictitiously and are not to be construed as real. Any resemblance to actual events, locales, organizations, or persons, living or dead, is entirely coincidental.

Originally published as 続・森崎書店の日々 in Japan in 2011 by Shogakukan Inc.

MORE DAYS AT THE MORISAKI BOOKSHOP. Copyright © 2011 by Satoshi Yagisawa. English translation copyright © 2024 by Eric Ozawa. All rights reserved. Printed in the United States of America. No part of this book may be used or reproduced in any manner whatsoever without written permission except in the case of brief quotations embodied in critical articles and reviews. For information, address HarperCollins Publishers, 195 Broadway, New York, NY 10007.

HarperCollins books may be purchased for educational, business, or sales promotional use. For information, please email the Special Markets Department at SPsales@harpercollins.com.

FIRST US EDITION

Designed by Jackie Alvarado

Library of Congress Cataloging-in-Publication Data has been applied for.

ISBN 978-0-06-327871-4 (pbk.)

24 25 26 27 28 LBC 5 4 3 2 1

More Days at the

Morisaki Bookshop

1

It's my day off from work, and I'm walking down the same familiar street. There's a feeling of calm in the air, like everything is at peace on this warm October afternoon. With a thin scarf loosely wrapped around my neck, I feel myself starting to sweat a little bit.

Even on a weekday around noon, the people I pass on the street walk at a leisurely pace and so do I. And from time to time, we come to a stop and disappear silently into one of the many bookshops along the way like we've been swallowed up.

The Jimbocho neighborhood is a little unusual for Tokyo because most of the stores there are bookshops. Each of the used bookshops has its own particular specialty: some carry art books, or play scripts, or philosophy texts; others handle rare items like old maps and traditionally bound Japanese books. Altogether, there are more than a hundred seventy stores. It's impressive to see all those bookshops lined up one after the other down the street.

If you cross the avenue, you'll find yourself in an area of offices, surrounded by tall buildings, but within its borders the neighborhood has done a good job keeping the rest of the city at bay. Only here are there rows of picturesque buildings. It's like the neighborhood exists in a different time, enveloped in its own quiet little world. Which may be why when you're walking around here, going wherever your fancy takes you, you look up and suddenly realize how much time has passed.

The place where I'm headed is on this corner. If you pass the street with the row of secondhand bookshops and turn onto the side street a little ahead, you'll be able to see it.

It's a used bookstore called the Morisaki Bookshop and it specializes in modern Japanese literature.

Once I turn the corner, I hear someone eagerly calling my name.

"Hey, Takako, come here!"

I look over and see a small middle-aged man looking my way, waving me over enthusiastically.

I hurry over to him and whisper my objection. "Didn't I tell you on the phone that you didn't need to wait for me? I'm not a little kid."

He's always like this, treating me like a child even though I'm a twenty-eight-year-old woman. It's obviously embarrassing, as you can imagine, to have someone shouting my name like that in the middle of the street.

"Well, it was taking you so long to get here. I got to worrying that you might've gotten lost."

"That's why I told you, you didn't need to wait for me in front of the shop. I've been here dozens of times. How could I possibly get lost?"

"Sure, I guess, but you know you can be a little bit absent-minded sometimes."

"You mean *you* can, don't you? Take a good look in the mirror sometime. You'll find a very absent-minded man staring back at you."

This is Satoru Morisaki, my uncle on my mother's side, and the third-generation proprietor of the Morisaki Bookshop. The original store, started by my great-grandfather back in the Taishō era, no longer exists. The current store was built almost forty years ago.

At first glance, my uncle Satoru might seem a little sketchy. He's always dressed in threadbare clothes, with slip-on sandals on his feet, and his shaggy hair makes you wonder if he's ever had a proper haircut in his life. And on top of all that, he's always saying off-the-wall things, and he ends up blurting out whatever he's thinking like a child. He is, in short, a tough man to figure out.

And yet, in this peculiar neighborhood, his odd personality and unusual appearance strangely seem to work in his favor: he's surprisingly well liked. It would be difficult to find someone around here who doesn't know my uncle.

His Morisaki Bookshop is an old-fashioned store, in a two-floor wooden building untouched by time, every bit the image of a vintage bookshop. The inside is cramped. You could get five people in there, but just barely. There's never enough space on the shelves; the books are piled on top, and along the walls, and even behind the counter where the cash register is. And the intense, musty smell particular to old bookshops penetrates everything. For the most part, the books on the shelves are cheap, running from around a hundred to five hundred yen, but the store also sells rarer things like first editions of famous writers.

The number of people looking for secondhand books like these has dropped since my grandfather's generation. From what I've heard, there were some extremely difficult times. It's only thanks to the customers who love the shop and have kept coming back over the years that it's still in business.

I first came to the shop more than three years ago.

Back then, my uncle let me come live on the second floor, and told me I could stay as long as I liked.

I can still vividly recall the days I lived here. At that time in my life, I was feeling desperate although the cause now seems insignificant when I look back on it. At first, I often lashed out at my uncle and locked myself in my room like some tragic heroine, crying all alone. Yet he patiently endured it all and offered me kind words and caring instead. As time went on, he taught me how thrilling reading can be, and how crucial in life it is to not hide from your emotions but to face them.

Naturally, my uncle was the one who introduced me to Jimbocho. At first, I was confused to look down the street and see just one bookstore after another.

"The great writers have always loved this place too," my uncle said, sounding like he was boasting about himself. "It's the best neighborhood of bookshops in the whole world." To be honest, I didn't get what he was talking about then. I couldn't see what there was to boast about.

But as time passed, I came to understand what he meant.

Jimbocho is brimming with charm and excitement. There's no other place like it in the world.

My uncle and I are still bickering back and forth in front of the shop when I hear a loud voice shout from inside, "Hey, what are you two doing?" When I peek in, I see a woman with a short, stylish haircut sitting at the counter, staring at us, with an irritated look on her face. That's Momoko.

"Quit dawdling out there and come in already, will you?"

She waved us in impatiently. She didn't seem to enjoy waiting in the shop for us by herself.

Momoko is Uncle Satoru's wife. You'd think she wouldn't be so different in age and appearance from my uncle, but she has such a straightforward and candid way about her that she seems much younger. My uncle is no match for her. Whenever she's around, he's always on his best behavior, like a little lapdog. It's only when she's there that you ever see that side of him.

Actually, Momoko lived apart from my uncle for almost five years, as a result of some unfortunate circumstances, but about a month ago she returned home safe and sound. Since then, she and my uncle have been running the shop together.

"So, Takako, what's new with you?" Momoko asks with a smile. She has such fine, straight posture that she somehow looks elegant even wearing just a sweater and a long skirt. I don't think I ever want to become someone who fills a room the way she does, but I do wish a little bit that I could have some of her grace.

"Things are good. Peaceful and calm. Work's going well. How are you?"

"I'm doing great," she says, flexing her arms to show off her biceps, like she's doing her Popeye impersonation.

"That's good to hear," I say, feeling a sense of relief. Years ago, Momoko had had a serious illness, and we're still watching her prognosis. My uncle is always very careful about Momoko's health, but it seems like his constant concern ends up irritating her.

"I've got some sweet daifuku mochi with me. Shall we have some?"

"Oh, maybe we should."

My uncle checks that Momoko has gone to the back and then complains to me in a whisper. "It's awfully cramped with Momoko here with me at the shop, but that's how it goes, I guess. It's just so much easier to work alone."

"But weren't you lonely when you were actually left all by yourself?" I'm only trying to tease him, but he gets all worked up and argues with me like a little kid.

"That's nonsense! I mean when she's back behind the counter, where am I supposed to go? These days, I'm just pacing back and forth by the entrance like a guard dog."

"Is that by any chance why you were standing out in front today?"

"Take a guess." He confesses this pitiful fact with a straight face, then leans forward like he's going to whisper in my ear. "But I've got more important things to tell you, Takako," he says.

"Like what?"

"The other day I got some pretty good stuff at auction. I haven't put it on sale yet at the shop, but for you I'll make an exception and let you have a little look."

He might've tried to sound reluctant, but I know there is no way he isn't going to show me those books. Yet I've been so thoroughly converted that I'm excited to see them. I almost wonder if this love of books is hereditary. I sometimes think that might be why I'm still coming so often to the shop on my days off from work.

"Show me!" I shout without meaning to. "I've got to see them!"

"Hey, I just made tea for you two." Momoko looks at us dumb-founded, with the teapot in her hands.

"This is a bookshop," my uncle says bluntly. "How are we not going to look at books? Right, Takako?"

"Right," I agree with a laugh.

My aunt gives us an annoyed look and grumbles, "You two are the worst."

This is my beloved Morisaki Bookshop. It's been an inseparable part of my life since the days I lived here.

In its own modest way, it's a place that holds so many little stories within its walls. Maybe that's the reason I keep coming back.

2

The Morisaki Bookshop bills itself as a store specializing in modern Japanese literature. The shop does stock some contemporary novels, but those are kept on the hundred-yen cart at the entrance. Inside the shop, there are basically only novels that date from the Meiji era to early Showa. (Which is why the interior is permeated by such a damp and musty smell, but that comes with the territory.)

Maybe it's because the shop deals with a special type of book that it tends to attract a lot of customers who are a bit *eccentric*.

Now I'm perfectly accustomed to them, but at first, they threw me off. It's not that they're hard to deal with. In fact, for the most part, they're perfectly harmless. They're just a little unusual, that's all. They come in now and then, hardly saying a word, lost in their single-minded search for a book. These customers, who are overwhelmingly elderly men, are, without fail, solitary figures. There's something about them that makes it impossible to imagine their everyday lives—so much so that if someone told me they were harmless ghosts, or some kind of otherworldly creature, I might actually be persuaded to believe it.

Whenever I visit the shop, I find myself weirdly concerned about whether they're still healthy enough to come in. I've never been close to them, but I can't help but hope they're well. I feel a kind of sympathy for them since we all love the same shop. And given the advanced age of most of these customers, I worry about them.

So, if they happen to come in when I'm helping out at the shop, I feel a secret relief when I see they're doing well.

Back when I was living on the second floor and working at the shop every day, the "paper bag man" was the one I worried about most of all. As his name suggests, he always came in carrying a tattered paper bag in both hands. Sometimes it was a bag from a department store, but occasionally it was a bag from one of the larger bookstores, like Sanseidō. He must have been going from store to store before he came to us, because the bag was often already full when he showed up. It looked quite heavy for his skinny arms. He invariably wore a dress shirt under a mouse-colored sweater.

If that was all, there wouldn't be anything so peculiar about him. The problem was that mouse-colored sweater. It wasn't simply frayed, no, it went far beyond that to the point where this article of clothing was so ragged that it was a miracle he was even able to wear it. Now, there was nothing about the old man that seemed unhygienic. In fact, he seemed neat and clean, aside from the absurd condition of his sweater, which looked like it had been dug up from some archaeological site.

The first time I saw him I was quite shocked. I snuck glimpses of him as he silently selected his books, and several times I felt the urge to shout, "Sir, you should be buying clothes, not books!" But he didn't seem to notice. He bought ten books, stuffed them into his paper bag, and left the shop without saying a word.

Ever since that day, I haven't been able to take my eyes off him when he comes in. Some weeks he comes in multiple times, but he's also gone a month without coming. He wears the same clothes every time. He's always gripping his paper bag of books in both hands. At the Morisaki Bookshop alone, on occasion he's bought books that cost ten thousand yen apiece. And yet his sweater only becomes more and more ragged. I couldn't help wondering who on earth this old man was. I was unable to muster the courage to talk to him, so I always ended up silently staring at his back as he walked out.

I tried asking my uncle about him once. "He's buying so many books—what if he has his own used bookstore in another neighborhood?"

"Nope. He's buying them to read them himself," he replied with certainty.

"Really? I guess you can tell the difference."

"That much I can tell whether I want to or not."

I guess that's how it goes. I could hardly distinguish one type of customer from another. But when a new customer walked into the shop, my uncle seemed to be able to tell at a glance whether they'd come to buy a book or if they had just wandered in on a stroll. He said his intuition was the result of years of experience.

"So," I said, letting my curiosity get the better of me. "What does that old man do for a living? Can you tell that too just by looking at him? It's not like he spends all his money on books and can't afford new clothes, right?"

"Hey." He spoke in the tone of voice you use to reprimand a child. "Your job isn't to start getting so nosy about the customers. The purpose of a bookshop is to sell books to people who need them. It's not right for us to start wondering what kind of job people have or what sort of life they lead. It's not going to make these older customers feel very good if they know the salespeople have been prying into their lives."

When I thought about it, my uncle's view seemed like a perfectly legitimate way of thinking about a business that caters to its customers. Even though he was usually making little jokes and chuckling to himself, after running a used bookshop for so many years, when something needed saying he came right out and said it. In moments like that, he could be kind of cool.

Anyway, that's the reason why the paper bag man's origins remain a mystery to us.

———

These eccentric customers each have their own distinct reasons for searching for books. It's truly fascinating. I'm always impressed by the wide range of circumstances that lead people to seek out second-hand books.

Take, for example, people who set out to collect rare books, without regard to genre, era, or region. They simply accumulate unusual volumes. When a well-known collector came into the shop, he seemed dissatisfied with what we had in stock. On his way out of the store, he said something that left me dumbfounded. "It doesn't matter if it's a masterpiece. If the volume isn't rare, it's worthless to me."

And then there are what we call the brokers. They acquire valuable books at as low a price as possible and then sell them to another bookshop, pocketing the difference in price. Basically, their trade is buying books. For these customers, the quality of the work is secondary. They probably never even read them. There are others too, people who aren't interested in novels, but instead seek out the work of the obscure artists whose illustrations appear alongside a text. Some of those collectors will rely on the barest of leads in their single-minded pursuit of those pictures. And then there are the people who won't put anything that isn't a first edition on their bookshelves. Even if they want a book, they won't buy it until they can find a first edition of it.

The one who takes the cake is the old man who only showed up once during the period when I was living above the shop.

He wandered in at dusk and went straight to the shelf in the back where we keep the most expensive books. As he pulled each volume off the shelf, he looked only at the colophon (that's the last page of the book) and then put it back on the shelf. He repeated the same action again and again. Occasionally, his hand would pause, and he would stare intently at some spot on the colophon, nod a few times, and then chuckle to himself with an evil grin. To be honest, I found it pretty creepy.

After the old man had finally finished inspecting every book on the shelf, he suddenly walked out. I turned to my uncle, who was sitting next to me, grabbed him by the sleeve, and asked him what in the world that man was up to.

"Oh, he's looking for the author's seal," he said without looking up from the account books, as if there were nothing particularly unusual about this.

"He's a seal collector. They rarely come to the shop, but there are some pretty famous ones around here. I'm sure I told you about Nosaki, didn't I?"

"A seal collector?" I was puzzled by this unfamiliar term.

"Yeah, the seals are stamped on the colophon."

My uncle pulled a book with a rather old-looking binding from the shelf and showed me the last page. It was Osamu Dazai's *No Longer Human*. Near the left edge of the colophon, I could see "Dazai" had been stamped in red. My uncle explained that back when bookbinding was still generally done by hand, the author would verify the number of copies and give his approval to the printing by stamping the books with his own seal. He said that in general they were just stamped with the author's name, but there were some that incorporated elaborate, elegantly designed patterns.

All of which is to say that the old man was after the seals. I had never known about the existence of these seals until my uncle explained it all to me. But still, what was the point? Was he going to cut out all of these seals and paste them like stamps into an album so that every night he could stare at them with that big smirk?

"Yeah, something along those lines," my uncle said nonchalantly. "Well, I think some of them would hate to cut them out of the books so they just collect the volumes."

"That's totally insane."

There are people in this world whose hobby is astronomy and who find the vastness of the universe thrilling. And then, on the other hand, there are people whose hobby leads them to go to great lengths to collect these insignificant little seals. It's kind of hard to fathom.

"Uh-oh, Takako. You might be getting a little too worked up about this," my uncle said at the end, giving me a sideways glance. When he saw the perplexed look on my face, he burst out laughing.

"Hey, I'm back." And with this cheery greeting, Sabu appeared. He closed the door behind him with a loud noise and said something I didn't quite understand. "Ah, great weather, isn't it today? It makes me feel like reading Kōsaku Takii." Then he plopped himself down on the chair in front of the counter like it was his. My uncle, who was accustomed to this, said, "I'll put on the kettle," and started to make tea.

Of all the regular customers of the Morisaki Bookshop, Sabu was probably the most regular of them all. Although that didn't necessarily mean he was making all that much of a contribution to our sales figures. Only that he was the one who came in more than anyone else. More of a regular browser. A short and stout man with a friendly face who loved to talk. I didn't know exactly how old he was, but I'd say somewhere in his midfifties. Except for the area around his ears, he's spectacularly bald. He'll sometimes joke about it himself.

"Oh, where's Momoko today?" he asked my uncle, while he looked all over the shop for her. Of course, Momoko was wildly popular with the men who were our regular customers. She was such a good listener and a straight talker that she seemed to have stolen their hearts. The result has been a curious phenomenon: a sharp increase in the number of customers who come to see her. Sabu, of course, is one of the many she has in the palm of her hand.

"If you're looking for her, she's over at the other place," my uncle said, gesturing toward the doorway with his chin. Sabu immediately looked disappointed.

"What? That's a shame."

Momoko recently started helping out in the evenings at the little restaurant less than ten steps from the shop. After the head chef suddenly quit, the owner turned to Momoko, who was both a good cook and good at handling the customers. I don't know if this is true or not, but I heard that the restaurant was doing amazingly well, far better than before. When we said we were concerned that a hectic job like that might be too much for her health, she said, "I can handle this. It's my choice. You and Satoru worry too much."

Sabu wasn't paying any attention to me, so I had no choice but to say hello.

"Oh, Takako, you're here."

Even though I had been right in the middle of his field of view, he seemed just now to be noticing I was there. Ever since Momoko's return, his treatment of me had been openly shoddy. Before that, he had taken such a liking to me that it was actually becoming a bit concerning. He'd even been telling me I had to marry his son.

"I'm helping out today," I said.

"Helping out? What's a young person like you idly frittering away a weekday afternoon? Don't you have a real job?"

"That's rude! It's easy to take a day off at my office."

He giggled when I took offense. That's how Sabu was. He was nice, but he had a sharp tongue.

In this neighborhood, however, he had a reputation for being someone who knew everything that was going on. It's something he took pride in. So whenever he came by the shop, he always asked my uncle first about the other regular customers.

"How's Takigawa doing these days?"

"He hasn't been in recently. Before, he'd always come in once every couple of weeks."

"I hope he's not ill."

"It would be a relief if he dropped by sometime."

"How about Professor Kurusu? That guy's figured out how to deduct his book allowance from his research budget. A clever move."

"The professor was here two days ago."

"How about Yamamoto then? The other day, he was so proud that his book collection had hit fifty thousand books that I got a little annoyed. He was definitely boasting."

And so on . . . Inevitably, the conversation came down to this:

"Everyone's getting older, huh. If this shop doesn't find some new customers, it's doomed."

"You said it."

And then Sabu and my uncle would laugh together as if they'd said something funny. Those two went through the same routine every time. It was weird to me that they never got tired of it.

For a long time, I'd had my doubts about Sabu.

Like, who exactly was Sabu?

He always seemed to have free time. I had never once seen him busy. And even if the books he bought were not big-ticket items, he'd been buying books for an awfully long time. Unless he had an extremely large house, where on earth was he keeping all these books? The fact that he had a beautiful wife, who always looked nice in her kimono, was another mystery.

Which naturally brought up another question. What did Sabu do for work?

The more I thought about it, the more it seemed that Sabu was the most mysterious character around.

At the shop, Sabu was essentially no longer treated like a customer. My uncle probably wouldn't get upset if I tried asking him about it.

So, at some point while the two of them were still sipping their tea and talking about this and that, I interrupted.

"Sabu, may I ask you something?"

"Why so polite all of a sudden?"

"What do you do for work? You talk a lot about people idly frittering away their days, but aren't you the idlest of them all?"

It was as if Sabu had been waiting for me to ask this question.

He slowly turned up the corners of his mouth and smirked at me like a detective in a hard-boiled novel. It was incredibly annoying.

"You want to know?" he said as he leaned forward on the chair in front of me, bringing his face closer to mine.

"I do."

Even though I already regretted bringing up the subject, I nodded just like he wanted me to. Interacting with Sabu often led to these extremely irritating situations.

"Why do you want to know?"

"Actually, I don't really care."

"You won't reel me in like that."

"Ah, come on, enough already. Okay, I've just got to know. I can't take it anymore. If you don't tell me, I won't be able to sleep tonight. There, satisfied?"

"Really?"

"Sure. I really, really want to know. What on earth do you do for a living?"

I was getting tired of asking, when Sabu nodded with a satisfied look, leaned closer, and whispered, "I'm . . . not . . . telling."

I stood there with my mouth opening and closing over and over like a goldfish. When he saw my reaction, Sabu doubled over laughing, *mhahahahah*. "Wait . . ." He was truly an infuriating old man. He was totally mocking me.

"No, it was too perfect. A masterpiece."

"Hey, Uncle Satoru knows, doesn't he?"

"Ah, um, I do, sure . . ."

"Hey, Satoru! You can't tell her!" Sabu shook his head fiercely side to side, looking flustered as he tried to command my uncle not to tell me. "It's too soon to tell Takako."

"Whoops, my mistake."

"What are you talking about?"

"A man with more of a mysterious side has more charm, don't you think? That's why I'm not going to tell you. Your curiosity will grow and grow until it becomes an obsession, and you'll end up dreaming about me."

"Absolutely not. It doesn't mean anything to me at all anymore."

"Such a headstrong woman."

"No, I really don't care. I'll never ask you again," I said indignantly.

"Well, I think I should be going now. I've had my fill of teasing you, Takako," Sabu said. Then he downed the rest of his tea and walked out of the shop, cackling to himself as he went.

"Good grief, that guy," I said, dumbfounded.

My uncle seemed to agree. "Well, he's a strange guy."

This shop really does attract one strange guy after another.

3

Near dusk, my uncle suddenly started to get agitated. "Where's Roy?" he shouted, his ridiculously loud voice reverberating in our tiny shop. "I haven't been able to find him since I got back from my delivery!"

My quiet moment reading a book while I worked at the register was now ruined. "How should I know where he is?" I said sullenly.

As far as my uncle was concerned, it didn't matter if someone was trying to read, he had no problem striking up a conversation with them. The idea of leaving them alone never even entered into consideration.

It was always fun spending time at the bookshop, only it was a shame that my uncle had to ruin it by being noisy like this. Back when I lived here, my uncle would go to the hospital to undergo treatment for his lower back, so we didn't actually overlap much at the shop. But now we were almost always here together. Which meant that I had to interact with him constantly. It might seem harsh to think of my uncle as being in the way in his own shop, but he's the kind of person who gets riled up by the tiniest things, so these annoying outbursts happened at least once a day.

"Roy was here the whole day until I went out!" My uncle was walking around the shop making a commotion, then he chased me away from the chair behind the counter where I'd been sitting and started desperately looking around.

"I told you I didn't know. You must've left him somewhere."

"Roy is as precious to me as my own life right now. I would never do such a thing." My uncle was still rattling on, when he suddenly shouted and bolted up to the second floor.

"That Momoko!"

After a moment, my uncle came stamping down the stairs, clutching a brown-colored cushion to his chest. I can't think of any other adult I know who would make such a fuss over a single cushion like that.

Recently my uncle hadn't just been suffering from back pain, he'd also developed a case of hemorrhoids, which, according to him, made the long hours sitting in a chair "absolute torture."

Still, running a used bookshop means you spend the better part of the day sitting in a chair waiting for customers. It was going to be impossible for him to do his job in this condition. What saved him from his predicament was this: a cushion with a hole in the center, otherwise known as a donut pillow. The cushion was so good at easing the pain that my uncle had absolute faith in it. He said he couldn't just call it a cushion. That would be heartless. And because it was for his hemorrhoids, he started calling it Roy. He wasn't doing it to be funny. No, he was totally, absolutely, 100 percent serious.

"Ooh boy." My uncle placed Roy on his chair and then lowered himself onto it with the care you'd expect from a bomb squad in an action movie. Which didn't stop him from grumbling and cursing Momoko's name. Apparently, while my uncle was out making deliveries, Momoko had left Roy drying on the veranda just before she went to the little restaurant to help out. Which was why my uncle was now furious with her.

"Well, it's good you found it, isn't it?" I felt obliged to ask. My uncle was catching his breath after his brush with danger.

"It's tough getting older. All these little ailments pop up."

"Stop talking like an old man."

"I am an old man," my uncle said with a hangdog look on his face.

"Uncle, you're still in your forties," I said, exasperated. I wanted him to stay healthy forever and not let the whole hemorrhoids thing drag him down. "You're still young. You've got time. Old people are older than you."

"These hemorrhoids are hopeless." The only people who can understand the pain of hemorrhoids are the people who have them. My uncle spoke these words like he was reciting a maxim. I'm sure it must've been terrible. Any type of hemorrhoids come with a considerable amount of pain. But it was impossible to take what my uncle was saying as anything other than a joke. "That reminds me. Should I get one ready for you?"

"I'm fine, thanks. I don't have hemorrhoids at the moment," I replied brusquely. I was getting a little tired of him, and I decided not to pay him any more attention. Why would he be getting one ready for me? I had absolutely no idea what he was thinking. Did he plan on naming it Roy Jr.? This wasn't my uncle's only weird fixation or obsession. He had many, many others too. Every single one of them was annoying. For example, after his midforties, he started insisting that whenever they ate curry at home, it could only be the Vermont Curry brand, and only the "mild" flavor. When Momoko inadvertently bought the "medium hot" version, he spent the whole day pouting sullenly. According to Momoko, he became so irritating she wanted to give him a giant kick in the butt. I knew exactly how she felt.

Anyway, we'd found Roy, so I assumed my uncle would quiet down a little. I let out a sigh and tried to go back to the world of my book.

However, just as the thought crossed my mind, I saw an innocent smile appear on my uncle's face, and he sidled right up next to me with his chair. As incorrigible as ever, he couldn't resist poking his nose in again to interrupt me.

"So, Takako."

I said nothing.

"Whatcha reading?"

"What? Come on. Does it matter?" But whether I tried to ignore him or get angry, it had absolutely no effect on him.

"Hey, is that Sakunosuke Oda?"

He'd snuck a look at the copy of *Sweet Beans for Two!* in my hand, nodded, and gave me a knowing look.

"You like the book?"

"I do. It's actually my second time reading it. There. Are you satisfied now? I'm reading, please don't interrupt."

But naturally, my uncle made no attempt to listen.

"Now there's another writer with a tragic fate."

My uncle's eyes narrowed like he was staring off into the distance as he went on in this earnest tone. "Ah, Takako, you like Sakunosuke Oda too . . . But I'm sure you don't know anything about his life yet. That's such a shame."

At this point, it was already too late. I could tell how eager he was to tell me. I knew there was no way he'd let me go until I'd listened to the whole story. My uncle knew an extraordinary amount about Sakunosuke Oda—his whole life, not just his books. When he liked a writer, he loved nothing more than to read their autobiographies, memoirs, biographies, collected letters, etc. It had nothing to do with the business of running a used bookshop. He did it purely to satisfy his own interest. One thing he loved about books was that they could tell him what kind of lives the writers led, how they lived, how they loved, and how they left this world.

To me, there was something wonderful about that. However, my uncle really loved to make people listen to him recount all this as if it were something he'd witnessed firsthand. That's how I ended up hearing about the lives of a lot of writers, people like Osamu Dazai, Takehiko Fukunaga, Haruo Satō. Of course, the lives of writers whose names now belong to history can be fascinating. But the time has to be right. Sometimes I'm not in the mood to listen to all that. But my uncle doesn't care whether or not the time is right; once the switch has been flipped, he gets a glimmer in his eyes back behind his glasses, and he talks and talks until he's had enough.

I gave up and closed the book with a dramatic sigh (which had no impact on him at all). I'd lost my time to read. What can you do? In this case, I could only listen to what he wanted to tell me.

"Sakunosuke had a tragic fate?"

"That's right," he said.

"You get a sense of that somehow from his style."

"A lot of his work is based on his experiences." He nodded deeply, perfectly satisfied now that I was showing interest in what he was saying. Then my uncle began to recount the events of Sakunosuke Oda's life with great enthusiasm.

According to my uncle, Sakunosuke's life had been a series of hardships. He suffered from tuberculosis when he was a student, and his misfortunes piled up until he had to leave college. He fell passionately in love with a woman named Kazue, who worked at a café, and he set his sights on becoming a novelist, but his work failed to find recognition, and for a long time they lived a life of poverty, with all its daily hardships. But their suffering was not in vain; his books *Vulgarity* and *Sweet Beans for Two!* finally won him the recognition he'd long sought. His writing career was on a roll, but a few years later, his beloved wife, Kazue, fell ill and passed away.

He had enough turmoil in his life to be the main character in a TV show.

Having lost Kazue, Sakunosuke would often collapse in tears, regardless of what others might think. Kazue was the first person Sakunosuke had loved deeply, and the one who had loved him in return. Without her love to support him, Sakunosuke's life fell apart. His tuberculosis grew more and more serious. He must have sensed that death was near. Because when Kazue was on her deathbed, he'd cried as he told her he would follow in a few years. In the time he had left, he searched for solace in alcohol and coffee, as well as in the arms of other women. He coughed up blood as he wrote his novels.

My uncle told the story without a pause, as if he'd actually memorized the whole speech.

You could say he had a talent for it. As I listened, I was now completely entranced by the story, hanging on my uncle's every word.

"In his later years, Sakunosuke was so exhausted both physically and spiritually that he started taking methamphetamines to help him go on writing novels. His illness was so advanced that without them, he couldn't even hold a pen. His body had given out."

"And methamphetamines are a kind of stimulant, right?"

"It's hard to imagine now, but at the time it was easy to buy them at the drugstore. He'd inject them and work on his novel for days without sleeping."

"Yikes." That truly is hard to imagine now. Such a heartbreaking story, I thought, no matter how much times have changed.

"And he's not the only one. There were a lot of writers who regularly used methamphetamines. It was fairly well known, for example, that Ango Sakaguchi was a meth head."

"A meth head?" The words somehow sounded kind of cute, but it actually meant—

"Someone addicted to methamphetamines."

I heard myself say "Yikes" again.

"It's a terrible story," he said, shaking his head woefully. "But Kazue always remained in his heart. One of his masterpieces is the story of a man, driven to despair by the death of his wife, who ends up taking money from his company and betting like a madman on whatever horse is in the number one gate at the racetrack. The sole reason he's doing this is because his dead wife's name, Kazue, is written with the character for 'one.' We can't know for certain what Sakunosuke was thinking when he wrote the story, but there's no doubt it's connected to his intense feelings for Kazue, whose name, after all, begins with the same character."

"Yeah . . . it seems undeniable."

I have a weakness for stories like this. Just imagining what happened left me feeling somber.

"Even when he was dependent on drugs, even when he was coughing up blood, he went on writing novels. And when he had a massive lung hemorrhage and was taken to the hospital, he went on a rampage, demanding to be released because he needed to write. But later on, he ended up collapsing at the inn where he was living, and this time he didn't recover. He died in 1947 at the young age of thirty-three."

"Thirty-three? If he'd been healthy, he could've written so many more books," I said, overcome by a sense of loss. "I wonder what he would have written if he'd lived longer."

"But you could also say that he was able to write the novels he did precisely because he lived such a short time, and because death was always on his mind, as he burned through what remained of his life. He had that monstrous tenacity. When you think about it, there are lots of writers who had short lives. I suspect that they were able to write such amazing books because their lives were so short. Sakunosuke Oda didn't write many books, but he left behind some wonderful short stories. Whether that was for better or worse, we can't say. The only way to find out is to ask Sakunosuke in heaven."

My uncle looked deeply moved as he spoke these words, with his butt resting on the donut-shaped cushion.

"Is that right?" I mumbled. I glanced at the spines of the books lined up on the shelf. "If you think about it, most of the authors of the books here are no longer alive. It's a little bit strange, don't you think? Their books are still with us, and we read them to this day, and feel moved by them." It was true. So many of the people whose names lined the shelves here had long ago left our world behind. When I thought about it, I started to feel close to tears again.

"You're right. The way they shaped their feelings made them last. It's amazing, isn't it? And it's not just writers. All artists are incredible. We can learn so much from the work passed down to us from our ancestors."

I nodded enthusiastically in agreement. "It really is true."

At some point, I realized the sun had set. Outside the windows, the world was shrouded in blue shadows. It was nearly time to close the shop. Somehow or other, my uncle had won me over, and I was drawn into his story.

But it wasn't so bad after all, I said to myself, as I thought about the life of Sakunosuke Oda.

I think that my uncle tried to study these authors' lives in such depth because he was trying to learn something from them, and lurking behind that desire was the hope that he might find a clue to help him understand his own life.

From what I've heard, when my uncle was young, he went through a profound existential crisis. He agonized over it.

So, in his twenties, he worked in Japan to save up money to travel, then put on his backpack and went wandering all over the world for months at a time, solo. When the money ran out, he came back to Japan and started over again. I guess you could say he was one of those guys who are searching for themselves. It might sound embarrassing to put it that way, but for someone like me, who can't be bothered to do anything, the way my uncle was able to follow through on this plan without getting intimidated seems pretty cool.

When I visited his house in Kunitachi, he showed me a picture of himself from those days. It looks like it was taken when he had just started traveling. In the photo, he's still a young man in his twenties. Since that was right after I was born, I'd never seen what he looked like at that age.

In the picture, he's standing in a crowd in Nepal or India (my uncle couldn't remember), his face is stubbly, his cheeks are sunken in, and his skin tanned by the sun to a dark brown. He stares into the camera, the pupils of his eyes glinting darkly in the light.

When I saw the picture, I ended up shouting, "Wow. You look like a totally different person." I really wasn't exaggerating. He had such a different air about him, compared to the way my uncle is now.

"I was young then. That's almost thirty years ago."

"It's not just that. I don't know, there's something kind of amazing about you in that picture," I said, still staring intently at the photograph. That young version of my uncle seemed to be staring back at me. To think that that young man today made such a huge fuss because he couldn't find his cushion. Life is strange.

"Well, at the time, I was really troubled. When I wasn't traveling, I spent all my time reading." My uncle scratched the back of his head through his scruffy hair, chuckling to himself, like he was ready to laugh off the concerns of his former self.

"Every time I look at that picture, it makes me laugh," Momoko said with a little cackle when she rejoined us.

Somehow that was the only picture he took during the many years he spent traveling.

"I only took it because it was my first trip, and I got caught up in the moment. From then on, I didn't bring a camera when I was traveling," my uncle said dryly.

"Really? What a shame."

"Nah, what's the use of leaving a bunch of pictures behind?"

"I guess that's one way of looking at it. Is this around when you met Momoko in Paris?"

"I met your uncle later on, I think," Momoko said. "At that point, he didn't look so terrible. There was more gentleness in his eyes. If he'd looked like this, I wouldn't have let him near me."

"I know it's me, but I look terrible."

"This guy looks like he's going to kill someone." After they said this to each other, they both doubled over laughing. Momoko pinched his cheek, and my uncle let her, as they roared with laughter. (Momoko has a baffling tendency to pinch the cheeks of people she's close to.) They're such a weird couple.

"But back in those days, my father and I didn't see eye to eye. We were constantly arguing. I have to admit though, that I gave him nothing but trouble in those days. It's true."

"You and your father have totally different personalities."

"Definitely. Totally different."

My grandfather was a stern man. He hardly said a word and never uttered a joke; his brow was always deeply furrowed. To him, being stern was a virtue. He even thought of it as a point of principle. According to what my mother told me, his wife died soon after his first marriage. He was already nearly fifty when he married my grandmother. Normally, you might think that since he was older, he would spoil his children, but my grandfather was not that kind of man. My mother and my uncle had quite a strict upbringing. My grandfather stuck to his principles when it came to running the bookshop too. He was absolutely uncompromising in his approach to the business. They said he even used to chase away customers who had only come to browse. It was the complete opposite of my uncle's approach.

"But you ended up being the one who took over from Grandpa."

"Strange, isn't it? I hope he's not rolling over in his grave," my uncle joked.

"I'm sure he's out of his mind with rage. He's thinking, that kid doesn't know the first thing about running a used bookshop. He's making so much noise he's driving everyone around him crazy," Momoko said, and the two of them laughed their heads off.

There was no need to worry though. My uncle's personality might be the exact opposite of my grandfather's, but when it came to the important stuff, they were the same. That was for certain.

I gazed again at the photograph of my uncle on the desk. The person in that photo was a complete stranger to me. That glint in his eyes could've been anger, or doubt, or some vague sadness.

I gave a silent message to the younger version of my uncle in the picture:

It's okay. You're going to meet nice people. You won't have to be so sad anymore. Even if you suffer from back pain and hemorrhoids, you'll be beloved as the owner of a bookshop. So you don't have to worry anymore.

4

The Saveur coffee shop is a three-minute walk from the Morisaki Bookshop. Everyone in the neighborhood knows the Saveur, as you might expect of a place that's been around for fifty years. In the old days, many of the great writers who lived in Jimbocho often spent time there.

The stone-walled interior is dimly lit by lamplight alone, and it's filled with the rich aroma of coffee. The effect is quite soothing. Though it's normally bustling with customers, it never feels noisy. In fact, the sound of chatter blends in with the understated piano music playing in the background, and the result is somehow even more pleasant. Since my uncle brought me here that summer three years ago, I've loved the place's atmosphere and the taste of its coffee. I'm still a regular customer.

The owner of the coffee shop is an elegant man in his midforties with a long, slender face. At first glance, he might seem intimidating, but he's actually quite friendly and easy to talk to. When he smiles, he gets sweet-looking wrinkles around his eyes. As soon as I open the door, he calls out "Welcome!" from behind the counter where he's brewing coffee.

Tonight was no different. As soon as I opened the door, he greeted me warmly, just like he always did. "Hey, Takako. Welcome!"

"Good evening. Seems busy again today." I looked around the store as I said hello.

"Thank you. We're heading into the busy season for the coffee shop. It's when we make more money," the owner said as he polished a glass. He flashed a slightly mischievous smile.

"I guess when it gets colder, people crave coffee."

"So it goes."

Actually, it didn't matter if it was spring or summer; this coffee shop always seemed to be bustling. Still, there was a particular pleasure in drinking a good cup of coffee during the colder times of the year. I supposed the other customers must have felt the same way.

"So, are you meeting someone?"

"I am."

"Oh, how nice. Well, enjoy."

I smiled and bowed slightly.

The waitress came over right away, as if she'd been waiting for me, and led me to a seat by the window that had just opened up. As a matter of fact, this coffee shop was also the place where my boyfriend, Wada, and I would arrange to meet. His office was nearby, so it was a perfect spot. Whenever he was working late, I would pass the time by reading a book and having a cup of coffee. As usual, I had tucked a favorite book into my bag tonight. I took it out right away and started to read. The time I spend this way is quiet, but also exciting—waiting for the person I love to arrive. It somehow feels incredibly luxurious to sit in your favorite coffee shop, reading a book, waiting for your boyfriend.

I had read for about a half hour, waiting this way, when I heard the sound of someone tapping on the windowpane. Wada was standing outside the window. Our eyes met, and he waved. When I waved back, he turned and headed to the entrance.

"Sorry to keep you waiting." He sat down across from me, a bit out of breath, as if he'd come in a hurry. There was no dress code at his work, so he was dressed casually today as usual. For the most part, Wada's clothes followed the same set pattern: a jacket with slim-fitting pants or slacks. If you asked him, he'd tell you it was because it was "too much of a hassle to pick what to wear," but that chic style was really what looked best on him. Today, he was wearing a stylish black jacket with gray slacks that fit him perfectly.

"I just got here," I said with a smile as I shut my book.

"Oh, I hope so." Wada looked at me for a long time with a smile on his face. He just stared at me without saying anything. He kept staring at me for so long that I started to feel embarrassed, then I realized his attention was actually directed at the book in my hand.

"Is that a collection by Taruho Inagaki?" Wada asked with a tinge of admiration in his voice.

"Oh, um, well, yeah . . ." I said, struggling a bit to figure out why these were the first words out of his mouth after we hadn't seen each other in a week. Wada, however, didn't seem to notice my reaction at all.

"*One Thousand and One-Second Stories* is pretty good, isn't it?" he said.

"It is." Wada seemed so happy that I quickly regained my composure and agreed with him. "They're perfect to read in a place like this. They're short and kind of cute. And it seems like they'd go well somehow with a cup of coffee."

"You're right. Absolutely," Wada said enthusiastically. "For starters, even the titles are funny. 'How I Lost Myself' or 'How My Friend Turned into the Moon.'"

"They're so funny. I mean that's why I've read this book five times now."

Wada was a proper book lover too. He had a particular weakness for old Japanese novels. He was far more knowledgeable than I was, since I had only just begun to read seriously. And like most people who love to read he seemed interested in what other people were reading too. He was always curious about each and every book I read. Whenever it was something he loved, he would start smiling like this, and when it was a book he hated or hadn't read yet, he would grimace like a child in the cafeteria being served a dish they hated. The look on his face was so earnest that I would end up feeling embarrassed, as if I were guilty of some awful betrayal. To be honest though, I sometimes looked forward a little to seeing that look on his face. On this particular day, my book seemed to be a hit, and I didn't get to see Wada's sad grimace.

"That reminds me, the first day we met here, you were reading Taruho Inagaki."

"Wait, is that right? I remember I was reading a book."

"No doubt about it. I remember that day vividly."

Hearing Wada tell me that so emphatically made me feel embarrassed somehow. I tried to hide it by laughing.

My relationship with Wada started when we ran into each other here at the Saveur one night and ended up having coffee together. I knew him by sight because he was a customer at the bookshop, but this was the first time we had really talked. Looking back, I think that's when I first felt attracted to him. We've been close since then, but we didn't officially decide we were a couple until sometime before the summer. So, at this point we'd been going out for only a matter of months.

I've tried to call him Akira, which is his actual first name, but even now I still find myself calling him by his last name, Wada, the name I've been using from the first time we met.

It's thanks to the owner of the Saveur that things turned out this way. Which is why I still feel indebted to him.

Wada is an exceptionally courteous person. He hates to be in the spotlight any more than is necessary. In crowded places, for example, he tends to withdraw to the background, listening quietly to everyone talk with a smile on his face, throwing out a clever comment from time to time. That's the kind of person he is. But there's also something quirky about him. Suddenly his stubborn side will emerge, and he'll declare, "Today I want to eat calamari. I decided this morning, and my decision is firm. I won't let anything else into my stomach." He could be a difficult guy to read. But I adored the way he was a little bit weird.

We had different days off from work, and Wada's job got busy at the end of each month, when it was common for him to work on his regular days off. So, we could often only meet for a period of time like this in the evenings. Our mismatched work schedule was proving to be a substantial stumbling block in our relationship. We were both the kind of people who take their job seriously. There was no way for either of us to just cut out early and call it a day. So, the time we were able to spend together was, by necessity, limited. While I couldn't help being frustrated by this, I also knew that there was really nothing I could do about it.

At any rate, this was our first time seeing each other in a week. We were having a cup of coffee and talking about going to get something to eat soon when Takano made a rare appearance outside the kitchen.

Takano was the kitchen manager at the Saveur. He was a tall and gangly young man who had such a timid way of speaking that he came off as completely helpless. I'd heard that he wanted to open his own coffee shop one day and was being trained here by the owner.

"Nice to see you, Takano. It's been a while."

"Good to see you too, Takako, and, er . . . um, you as well, Wada."

Takano tended to be pretty shy around strangers, and it seemed that he was only slightly familiar with Wada and still not used to speaking to him.

"Good evening. It's Takano, right?" Wada replied with a warm smile. I could see from the look on Takano's face that this put him at ease too. Wada had a knack for this. He could talk to anyone easily and make them feel comfortable.

Yet even after we finished greeting one another, Takano continued to hang around for some reason, lingering nearby like a hyena eyeing a lion's leftovers. It was getting a little weird, so I asked him what was going on.

"Ah, no, it's okay. We can talk next time."

Just as he was mumbling his response, the owner called, "Hey, Takano!" from the other side, his voice radiating anger.

As soon as Takano heard him, he panicked and rushed back to the kitchen.

"What was that about?" I was left shaking my head as I watched Takano's spindly frame abruptly disappear into the back.

Wada looked equally confused. "He did seem to be acting kind of suspiciously."

"Still, acting suspiciously is hardly a new thing for him."

"In that case, I guess there's nothing to worry about."

After saying these rather rude things about Takano, we managed to convince ourselves, and left the Saveur.

We sauntered into the Sanseidō bookstore at closing time, then after we'd finished our meal at a nearby set-menu restaurant that Wada liked, we went on a little walk around the neighborhood. We both had to work the next day. I had an early meeting in the morning, so we decided we'd both go home afterward. Wada walked me to the station.

Wada's apartment building was located about a fifteen-minute walk from the neighborhood of used bookshops. I'd only been there a few times, but the first time I went it gave me quite a shock. "My apartment's a mess," Wada tried to warn me repeatedly on our way there, and it truly was.

The moment I first set foot inside the door, I saw the leftover bento containers from the convenience store and discarded clothes scattered all over the floor. His substantial number of books were not only stored on the bookshelves, but had been left all over the sofa and the table. The kitchen area was even more disastrous. The sink was overflowing with dirty plates and frying pans. It was an appalling sight. While it would be an exaggeration to say there was nowhere to step inside, at the very least there was nowhere to sit. The closet door had been left half open, and there were huge cardboard boxes piled on top of each other inside. I peeked in the boxes, with his permission, and found lots of secondhand books. It looked like there might be some valuable ones there, but they'd been thrown in so haphazardly that it looked like it would be an ordeal just to get them organized. In any case, given how disorganized they were, it probably would have been better to have the Morisaki Bookshop pack it up and take the whole pile away.

"I'm really sorry. I'd planned to clean up, but this week has been so busy at work, I just didn't have time."

I'd been anxious about coming to his place, but my anxiety vanished once I saw what it looked like. I was laughing about it to myself for a long while. I felt like I'd seen an unexpected side of him, but it was so unexpected I didn't know what to make of it.

"Well, I guess this is just what single guys' apartments look like," I said.

Wada, who had been panicking, now seemed to relax a bit. I'd been surprised because it was Wada's apartment, but this level of disorder is pretty common in general. Of course, it would be nice if he'd cleaned it for the first time his girlfriend came over, but . . .

"What did you do when your last girlfriend came over?" I asked nonchalantly.

"Ah, well, she always cleaned up for me whenever she noticed. She was the kind of person who liked things to be clean," Wada said, smiling grimly.

I suddenly regretted asking the question. You ask too many questions, I said to myself.

Wada had brought that woman several times to the Morisaki Bookshop back then. She had beautiful features and a tall, slender figure. At the time, I only knew them by sight, so I would casually look at them and think, "Oh, what a beautiful couple." Now that the situation had changed, I wanted to take that image and stick it in the cardboard box in the closet along with all the books. Burning with petty jealousy, I decided at that moment that I would clean his apartment. I wouldn't let that woman beat me. So, that afternoon, while Wada stood by unsure what to do with himself, I transformed into one hell of a cleaning machine.

That was how I ended up spending the night at Wada's place.

In Wada's arms, I became aware of something within the core of my being. And it felt like that core was being touched. It was probably the first time in my life that I'd ever felt that way.

At the same time, I worried whether Wada could really be enjoying himself with an ordinary person like me. In Jimbocho, I had met so many truly fascinating people, starting with my uncle, (even Sabu, I had to admit, was fascinating in his own way), but the flip side of that was that it made me realize just how dull and ignorant I was. Which left me worrying that Wada would soon realize it too.

I wanted to spend more time with him, to share all kinds of things together. But I wasn't sure if Wada felt the same way. I'm terrible at romance, forever a late bloomer. That might be to blame for my last relationship, which came to a terrible end. It turned out I was the only person who had thought we were going out to begin with. Now, I was 100 percent certain that Wada wasn't that kind of guy, but I still couldn't tell how much he needed me.

Wada wasn't the type to show his emotions. So I sometimes became extremely worried trying to figure out what he was thinking. What was he looking for in a girlfriend? Did he love me more than he'd loved his previous girlfriend? It's not like I was as beautiful as she was. These thoughts weren't getting me anywhere; they just kept going around and around in my head. But one thing was quite clear. I knew what I felt, and I wanted to express it to him in my own words. And what I definitely didn't want to do was just muddle my way through that feeling or the relationship I'd begun with him.

Reading had started to affect me in ways I hadn't expected. I had been touched by the kinds of love I read about in books, and that had strengthened my belief that I needed to take my own affections more seriously.

"*It gets so* much colder at night."

"Yeah."

We were slowly walking up the slight hill that leads to Ocha-nomizu Station. Jimbocho Station is much closer, but we had purposely gone the long way. Unlike the neighborhood of bookshops where everyone goes to bed early, this side of the street was still lit up with its many restaurants and shops selling musical instruments. There were many walking down the street and a constant stream of cars.

I wanted to stay with him.

But I had to go home.

In my head, the same thoughts kept coming back over and over.

I was watching Wada out of the corner of my eye as he walked beside me. Wada took each step so smoothly, without any wasted movement. His footsteps hardly made a sound. It was just like him. Was he feeling a little sad too? The expression on his face looked the same as always.

As we continued our walk, we had a conversation about the right book to read before going to sleep. Wada surprised me by saying he couldn't sleep if he read in bed. He told me with a straight face that if you had to read something, then the phone book would do. After a long deliberation, I suggested Kōtarō Takamura's book, *The Chieko Poems*.

"Though I think it would be a waste of a great book because you can't actually read that much before you go to bed."

"Somehow neither of us can come up with a proper answer," Wada said with a smile. "But I see that *The Chieko Poems* is a really important book for you."

"I mean I don't know of another book that's so filled with love."

"I agree. Chieko's mental illness only strengthened his love for her, and as if in response, his poems became more beautiful."

An excerpt from *The Chieko Poems* was included in my textbooks in school, so of course I was familiar with it. But once I started to read the book from the beginning, I was surprised by how moving it was. The days Takamura spent with Chieko, all the happiness, worry, sadness, and pain of their love, all the emotions, from their first meeting to their wedding, the outbreak of her illness, and her death, were turned into lines of poetry. There's a light within those poems that shines so brightly it's almost blinding.

I think that probably for a lot of people, a great many actually, *The Chieko Poems* is an important, even irreplaceable book. And I am certainly one of those people. Whenever I read it, I'm overcome with emotion. So much so that I no longer feel the need to put it in words.

That's why I only allow myself to read the book when I'm really compelled to. Because I want to hold on to the part of me that finds reading this book so moving. Whenever I read it, I always end up crying. No matter how many times I reread it, the tears always well up. I get tears in my eyes, just thinking about the book.

I think about how wonderful it must be to be able to put one's thoughts into words like that.

As the thought crossed my mind, I realized the station was already in view. It was time to say goodbye.

We said good night and went our separate ways. This was the most painful moment in the day for me. Try as I might, I can't find another word to describe it.

I stood for a moment in front of the turnstiles and watched Wada gradually recede into the distance. I thought that I might read a little bit of *The Chieko Poems* before bed. It had been a while. I thought about it all the way home.

5

Day by day, we went deeper into autumn. Winter was closing in. The dry wind was cold enough to make us shiver. Along the road, the trees had just begun to change color. Before we knew it, the sun would set earlier with each passing day, and the nights would grow longer and deeper.

This was my favorite time of the whole year, the period before winter had truly arrived, the time to mourn the passing season. It made me want to stand still and stare up at the pale blue sky and its soft light. That's why lately my morning routine had been to walk to work with my gaze turned to the sky.

I was working at a design studio in Iidabashi, the same company that had hired me when I moved out of the bookshop. It was a very small firm whose main business was designing pamphlets and leaflets. If you include the time in the beginning when I was part-time, I'd been working there almost three years.

Since many of our jobs were basically solo projects, we didn't have strictly defined hours or workdays, and as long as we maintained basic office etiquette, we were relatively free to do as we wished. At the company where I worked before, our personal relationships were kept secret, and they definitely even had cliques, all of which I was truly terrible at navigating. In part because my new firm was small, I could keep clear of those sorts of entanglements. My income was significantly lower than at my last job, but I was able to work at my own pace, and I felt like the new place was definitely a better match for me.

Staying late at night at the office slogging away at work isn't my favorite thing to do, so I was usually the first one to arrive in the morning, and I would try to finish up early in the evening. I'd have conversations with my coworkers, but I didn't get involved with them any more than was necessary. I rarely met them outside of work.

Perhaps because of all this, on one of the rare occasions when I was invited out for drinks with my coworkers, one of them said to me, "You kind of keep to yourself, don't you?" The others seemed to have formed the same impression of me. In their view, I didn't talk much, and I always went straight home early in the evening. It caught me a bit by surprise, but when I thought it over, it seemed a major reason for this might be that I had found a place where I felt at home.

Before I mostly would just go back and forth between home and work. I didn't have any real hobbies or any strong attachment to anything. I wasn't especially unhappy, but I did have the slight sense that my life was missing something. Looking back, I think I always felt that way and didn't know what to do about it. But I didn't feel that way anymore. Of course, it would be foolish to say that I felt perfectly fulfilled right now. It was just that when I thought about it, I no longer really felt that anything was missing.

There were places I wanted to go and people I wanted to see. And there was a place that was always ready to welcome me back.

I can't think of anything more wonderful than that.

I was able to do my job working at my own pace. I liked the job itself, and things at the office weren't too bad. I felt confident that things were headed in the right direction.

But more recently, I did run into a little bit of trouble. Deep down it was a trivial matter. If I told anyone about it, they'd probably laugh it off like it was the punchline of a joke. But the truth is it was pretty upsetting to me.

It all started one day at lunch. The company didn't have a cafeteria or a set lunchtime. It was up to each person to spend their lunch break as they saw fit. I generally went to a nearby café. It was empty even at lunch, and I never saw anyone from work there, which made it the place I felt most comfortable eating.

One day, however, I unexpectedly bumped into a senior colleague. He was a guy who had a sarcastic, condescending way of talking to people. I'd already had a feeling that he was someone I'd have a hard time with. So, I casually said hello and tried to find another seat, but he called out to me.

"Hey, come sit here."

I didn't have any other choice but to sit with him. As I might have expected, it was not exactly festive at our table. It was partly my fault for not making an effort to keep the conversation going, but I really didn't know how to respond when he went on talking and talking, boasting and complaining about work. "The problem is our clients are too idiotic to know better. I need a bigger job to put my talents to work. With our current projects, I barely feel like putting in fifty percent of what I'm capable of." We spent the whole lunch break with him going on like this with a revolting look on his face. In the end, I could only muster a simple "uh-huh" in response.

That should have been the end of it. I thought to myself, it's just one of those things—you run into someone you don't like; today's not your lucky day. But afterward, he started looking for ways to talk to me whenever he could. Even at the office, if I was busy working at my computer, he'd go out of his way to come over and start talking to me. If I pretended not to hear him and kept on working, he'd come over and hit me on the back to force me to pay attention to him. Then he started asking me out to lunch as if that were perfectly normal. I had absolutely no idea what could possibly motivate him to want to spend another dull hour in my company. And in my position, I couldn't very well turn him down every day, so I got stuck going back to that same café with him many times after that day. Of course, all that was waiting for us was a total waste of time.

What was the point of it all? What did he find amusing in all this? Was this just some new form of harassment? I was getting more and more irritated.

On the fourth time he forced me to take my lunch break with him, in a pause between complaining and boasting, he suddenly asked me, with a mouthful of sandwich, "So, what do you do on your days off?"

"I . . . um . . . go to secondhand bookshops a lot." I was caught so off guard that I made the mistake of giving him an honest answer.

"Why? What would you want to go to a place like that for? What are you, an old man?" He burst out laughing like I'd just told him the funniest joke he'd ever heard. *You have no right to ask me what I do on my days off!* I said to myself, but then I remembered he was still above me at work. There was no way for me to say that out loud.

"How about we go for a drive on your next day off?"

After another surprise attack, I felt more and more upset. "Um, why would we do that?"

"What do you mean 'why'? If you're not busy, wouldn't it be nice?"

"No . . . I have, um, plans."

"Plans?"

"I just told you about the bookshops."

"Come on. Nobody goes to bookshops that often."

"People who like them do though. There's nothing wrong with that," I replied. I was definitely getting annoyed. He scratched his head in confusion and took a deep breath. He let out a sigh rich with pity, like a teacher coming across a high school dropout in the guidance counselor's office.

"Do you enjoy life?" he asked.

"What?"

"I mean it's like you're always under a dark cloud. You can't keep up a conversation. It's like what's the point in talking to you? Even when I try to help you out and invite you places, you start squirming and say something about used bookshops or whatever. You need to get a more positive attitude, or you'll end up wasting your life."

After this parting shot, he didn't give me a second to reply before sniping, "This is boring." Then he got up and walked out. For a moment, I couldn't move at all. I just sat there stunned, with my mouth hanging open.

"Oh, how annoying!"

That night, I went to see Momoko at the little restaurant where she was working and sipped sake as I went rattling on about the incident at lunch. Recently, I'd started to frequent the restaurant, drawn by Momoko's cooking. Mr. Nakasono, the restaurant's owner, was an affable guy who had a way with words. In that sense, he and Momoko were a pretty good match. But maybe because he couldn't keep track of all the names and faces of his customers, Mr. Nakasono just could not remember my name. Every time I came into the restaurant, he would start calling me "Mikako" or "Yukako" or something like that. No matter how many times I corrected him, the next time he saw me, he always mixed it up again. I finally resigned myself to it.

That night, after being called "Teruko," which is quite a long way from my actual name, I shook with rage before quickly deciding it didn't matter.

On the other side of the counter, Momoko was busy at her work, looking quite at home in her apron. "Hey, don't come into someone's place of business jabbering on when you've had too much to drink," she said, like she was telling off a drunk customer.

I was, on this rare occasion, actually rather drunk.

"But it's so incredibly annoying. Of course it's annoying to have to hear that from him, but the most annoying thing of all is that I couldn't even respond."

"Yeah, I get it, sure. It's annoying. I get it."

The drunker I became, the angrier I felt about what I saw as his high-handed attitude. And what made matters even worse was that his name, by some twist of fate, was Wada. That was another thing I found extremely unpleasant.

"I wouldn't call it a twist of fate. Wada's a common name. It's not as if it was his choice to be named Wada," Momoko said in disbelief.

"But I can't stand it. I mean when you think of him, doesn't Wada end up popping into your head too?"

"So you've been thinking about this guy, have you?" Momoko said, with a malicious grin.

"That's not what I mean. I mean like when we're talking about him now," I said, taking offense.

"Well, I guess it is inconvenient. Shall we call him Wada #2 then?" Momoko said, giving him an impromptu nickname. "So, basically you're saying Wada #2 asked you out and you didn't realize it?"

"No, I knew, but I didn't know why he was suddenly talking to me about all that."

"He asked you out because he thought you wanted him to, and then you got angry at him."

"It doesn't make sense, does it? Like is that how people really see me?"

"Well, that's how Wada #2 did," Momoko said dryly. She shrugged, as if to say, Don't get mad at me. "But you can be a little like that, you know, Takako."

"Like what?"

"You know, careless."

"What do you mean, careless? I wasn't doing anything."

"Sometimes that's the same thing. And sometimes that can invite an even more thoughtless response."

That startled me. I'd been guilty of that in the past. "I guess you're right . . . I did run into some trouble that one time."

"Ah, are you referring, for example, to the case of the girl who locked herself away inside the secondhand bookshop?"

"What, that? Please let's not start giving the events of my life weird case names."

Momoko burst out laughing. "But although you can be a little slow . . . and careless . . . and, well, tactless, I do love how sweet you are." Momoko stared at me with a smile. Her soft, short hair gleamed in the fluorescent light.

"I can't quite tell if you're complimenting me or insulting me."

"Nah, I'm complimenting you, more or less," Momoko said, laughing out loud again. "Coming back to what you were saying before though, even if Wada #2 saw you like that, it doesn't necessarily mean that he truly saw you for who you are as a person. He just saw you from his own preconceived point of view. The point is, if you'd been a little more aware, you could've steered clear of someone like that who was going to put you in a difficult position."

"That's easier said than done. He's above me at work."

"Which is why you've got to do your best to give off an aura that says you're not interested in getting any closer to this guy. You can project that. And even as dumb as he is, he'll get the message."

"Oh, I really am terrible at that sort of thing."

"That's what I meant when I said you were so sweet. And I want you to be yourself. I like you just the way you are," Momoko said as she reached across the counter and patted me on the back.

"What do you mean?"

"You might often end up on the losing side that way, but isn't it better to be true to who you are?"

"I guess." I didn't really understand what she was talking about, but I figured she was saying she wanted me to remain the same.

"But there are people like that, you know, people who are so self-centered. To someone like that, it doesn't matter if it's you or somebody else who's there with them."

It was painful to hear, but I knew she was right. I'd had a bad experience like that in the past. I thought that person had chosen me, but in fact, it wasn't true. He would've been satisfied as long as it was *someone like me*. It was deeply upsetting, because it felt like my very identity was being negated. On the other hand, it's clear that I bore some of the responsibility.

"There are all kinds of people in this world. A person like Wada #2, he's the main character in the story of his life. Of course, personally I'm not that interested in reading a book about that Wada #2." Momoko stuck out her tongue like a naughty little kid.

"Listen, life is short. In the story of your life, you've got to avoid people like that. Choose to be with the people who really choose you, people who see you as irreplaceable. That's the story you want—you know what I'm saying?"

"I do. I know exactly what you mean."

I really did feel like I understood. It seemed to me to be deeply connected to what I'd been thinking lately about my relationship with Wada. Someone who chose me for who I am. Was that how Wada (and, of course, I'm not talking about Wada #2) thought of me? Wada was the only one for me. There was no way someone else could take his place.

"That's good. Take it to heart. It's a little advice from one of your elders."

"Okay."

Our conversation had taken a strange turn, but I knew what Momoko had told me then was true. I nodded obediently, accepting what she'd said.

A few days later, a last-minute request for edits came in from a client, and it brought with it so many new deliverables that it led to a series of hectic days at the office. Thanks to that, I guess, though maybe "thanks" isn't the right word, I didn't have any time to give Wada #2 another thought.

Then, one night, after things had started to look up again at work, I left the office feeling exhausted and found myself walking automatically to the Saveur. It's not because I was planning on meeting Wada there, I just had an overwhelming urge for a cup of coffee. You're a real addict now, I thought. I laughed a little to myself as I made my way to the coffee shop.

Opening the door, I heard the familiar sound of lively conversation, and I realized that Sabu was there. And of course, there he was, sitting at the counter, talking to the owner.

"Hey, good to see you." After a brusque greeting, I sat down beside him and ordered a blend coffee and Japanese-style Napolitan spaghetti with a salad because I was feeling incredibly hungry.

The owner turned to the kitchen and yelled, "Hey, Takano! One Napo on the double!"

"Okay!" Takano replied a bit sheepishly.

"By the way, that idiot has been trailing around after you, Takako.

Is he talking nonsense to you again?" the owner asked, maybe thinking about Takano's odd behavior the other day.

"No, not particularly."

"If he bothers you, feel free to give him a smack on the head."

"Sorry, I don't think I could do that," I said, taken aback. It made me wonder what it must be like for Takano to work there, having to put up with such harsh treatment.

Sabu was in fine form as usual, chatting about one thing or another as he sat beside me.

"What's wrong—are you tired?" Sabu asked, more or less admitting he was bored when I failed to keep up my end of the conversation.

"Yeah, things have been a bit busy at work. You look well though, Sabu, as always."

Sabu giggled. "You need to take a vacation. I, on the other hand, am so powerful, so robust, that I don't need time off."

I guess it must've been my imagination then that he seemed to be on a permanent vacation.

"I take days off all right."

"Is that so? And then you're always hanging around Satoru's place. If anyone, it's Satoru who never takes a day off. Momoko came back, but nothing's changed. If he keeps it up, she'll run off again. I'm always taking my wife on trips or taking her out to eat, bringing her to all kinds of places and whatnot to keep her happy."

"After all, when she's unhappy, she throws away your books," the owner muttered, sending Sabu into a rage.

"Shut up, old man!"

"The only old man here is you."

"Ah, that's true. I'm the old guy," Sabu said, slapping his bald head. Then he burst out laughing like an idiot. To my surprise, the owner, who had been polishing glasses with a blank expression, couldn't keep from laughing a little. These two had a weird relationship. It was hard to know if they liked or hated each other.

Nonetheless, what Sabu said touched on something I'd been concerned about for a while. Momoko had come back, but despite the fact that they now had time to spend together, my uncle was just working nonstop. Even on the days the shop was closed, he would go out in his run-down little van, traveling long distances to buy books. He didn't seem to be setting aside any time at all for them to spend together. He was extremely worried about her health, and yet I couldn't see any sign that he was actually trying to take care of her.

As I sipped my coffee, I thought about how hopeless my uncle was and sighed. "My uncle should take some time off. What with his hemorrhoids and all."

"Right, think of his hemorrhoids. He ought to go to the hot springs and really relax. What if he took your aunt with him?"

It sounded like it might be a good idea. I forgot all at once about feeling tired, and was now bounding with energy.

"That's great. That's an amazing idea."

My uncle was too busy at the shop to realize it, but what if I offered them a little trip as a simple gift to thank them for all they've done for me? Momoko was just saying that their wedding anniversary was in November. It might be a little early, but I could say it was my present for them. I could take care of the reservations for the inn and the train tickets for my uncle, because that was too much of a hassle for him. That ought to make both of them happy.

"Ah, wouldn't that be nice?" the owner said. "It would be good for Momoko, of course, but even Satoru should take a break every once in a while. He might seem carefree, but when it comes to the bookshop, he's so devoted to his work that he might be taking it too far."

I felt encouraged by what he'd said. And at that moment another idea popped into my head that made me even happier. I was getting extremely excited.

"Sabu, on occasion you say something smart."

"Hey, what do you mean, 'on occasion'?"

"I ought to thank you though," I said, sincerely expressing my gratitude.

It was rare to see Sabu looking slightly embarrassed by the attention. He turned away and mumbled, "Okay, that's enough," chewing his words. He seemed unaccustomed to being thanked, maybe because he was always needling people.

"Thank you, Sabu." I pushed it a little more and said it again.

"No, really, that's enough." Sabu looked truly embarrassed now as he brought the coffee to his mouth, mumbling.

He looked unbearably funny.

"Look at you laughing all the time. You haven't got a care in the world."

"Though someone told me recently that I was an extremely gloomy person."

"Must be something wrong with his eyes. The only time you've ever been gloomy was back in your sleep monster days. Now you're Miss Carefree."

"Hey, you might be right. Thank you, Sabu."

"I told you to quit that. It makes me all itchy. If you keep going, I won't say another word!" Sabu said, scratching all over his back.

"Takako, I see you too have figured out how to tease Sabu. And here is your Napolitan." The owner placed my spaghetti with plenty of ketchup on the table in front of me.

I ate in a trance.

By the time I was full, my fatigue had vanished, and the anger I'd felt toward Wada #2 had long since disappeared.

6

My uncle and I got into a fight.

It was the first time in all the years we'd known each other that we had ever had a real fight like this. And yet the reason for this fight and the issue we fought over were fundamentally stupid.

It began with the aforementioned trip.

After I hit upon the idea at the Saveur, I immediately went home and selected several promising-looking hot springs resorts online and arranged everything so that once they made their choice, I would make the reservations.

Then on the afternoon of my day off, I headed over to the Morisaki Bookshop, bubbling with excitement.

"Wait, aren't these all weekdays?"

"It's fine. There are a lot more openings than on the weekends. And you could use some time away from the shop."

"But I can't close the bookshop."

I'd been expecting that response. "I knew you'd say that," I told him proudly. "I will look after the shop for you."

The truth is that I had a bit of an ulterior motive for my plan. With Satoru and Momoko away, they'd naturally need someone to look after the shop. I had secretly been wanting to spend a few days there. Of course, if I'd asked my uncle, I could've stayed on the second floor above the shop whenever I wanted, but that would be a completely different thing. Even if it was for a short stay, I wanted to manage the shop from morning till evening, and then spend the night in that room upstairs that made me nostalgic now. That way

I could soak it all in, and there'd be no one to shout, "Where's Roy?" and ruin the mood. My uncle could let his weary body get some rest, and to top it off, I could enjoy myself. It was two birds with one stone—at least it should've been.

"No way. You've got your own job, Takako."

"My days off match up, so it's okay."

"Well, we'll take you up on your generous offer then, Takako," said Momoko, who had been listening nearby. "How thoughtful of you." She had a gleam in her eye and seemed as pleased as I'd expected.

"Hey, don't just decide for both of us," my uncle grumbled.

"What's wrong with the idea? It's good to take a day off every once in a while. Besides, Takako's gone to a lot of trouble. She wants to do this for us." Momoko gave his cheek a good pinch as if to say, *What a hardhead.*

"Nope. It's out of the question," my uncle insisted stubbornly, even as his cheek turned red. "I mean, what'll we do if something goes wrong?"

"So you won't even go on a day the shop's closed?"

"That's right. Next week I promised Yoshimura I'd go to buy stock from his place in Saitama."

"Then a regular weekday should be fine. If it's just a day or two, even I can take care of things. Please have a little faith in me."

"Absolutely not," my uncle flatly refused.

"But why not?"

"It's hopeless," Momoko said, throwing her hands up. "When he gets like this, there's no sense in talking to him."

I'd prepared myself for a little resistance, but not this level of stubbornness. Although I might have had a slight ulterior motive for my offer, I truly wanted to show how grateful I was to them by giving them some time off. I stared at my uncle with resentment, feeling profoundly disappointed.

"You really hate the idea that much?"

"Hate it? What's out of the question is out of the question."

"God, I can't stand you!"

"It's out of the question!"

"Stop acting like little kids, you two," Momoko interjected, looking at us in disbelief. "If that's how you feel," she added, "then Takako
and I will go together like last time. Besides, I'll have more fun with
her than I will with whatever this is."

"Then what's the point?"

He really was pouting like a spoiled child. But I can be stubborn
too. And I was going to make him take time off and go on that trip.

For a very, very long time, my uncle and I went back and forth,
repeating these meaningless replies again and again—"Go!" "Out of
the question!"—until the original intention faded away, and we were
just butting heads, each refusing to give in.

I don't know if there's ever been a more meaningless fight in the
world.

In the end, I shouted, "That's enough!" and walked out of the
shop, fuming. I got carried away and shut the door behind me as
hard as I could, and the sound it made was so much louder than
I expected that I was taken aback, but I walked away pretending
nothing had happened.

The day after all that, I met up with Wada. It was our first time seeing each other in four days. Naturally, we'd arranged to meet at the
Saveur. However, on this particular day, Wada showed up with an
oddly stiff expression on his face. Then, as he was about to take his
seat, he suddenly asked, "Can we talk for a second?"

I flew into a panic. What on earth could it possibly be? I'd been
expecting us to spend some quiet time together tonight, so this caught
me completely by surprise. "Huh? What is it?" I asked nervously.

"Could we change tables?" he asked, also looking quite nervous. That made me feel even more uneasy.

"Um, is this a good talk . . . or a bad talk?" I asked, preparing myself for the worst.

"A good talk? No, I don't think so."

What could I do? What had I done? As I started to panic, the thought of my stupid fight with my uncle vanished from my mind.

"W-w-where are we going?"

"Um, I don't know. What should we do? This spot is fine, actually. It's nothing important."

I had no idea anymore what was going on. A minute ago, he seemed so nervous, now he was telling me it was nothing important. When he started, for a second I thought he might even be about to talk about getting married. Lately, my mother had been pestering me on the phone, always asking, "When are you getting married?"

I just realized I'd reached the age where you start to make your parents worry about that sort of thing. But this was apparently going to be a bad talk? It had to be about that. It was too terrible for words. I still wanted to be with Wada. I was still dreaming of being with him forever and ever. Or maybe he was keenly aware of that and felt pressured.

"You won't laugh, right?" Wada asked earnestly, heedless of the fact that my mind had gone blank.

"I can't be sure until I hear what you have to say, but I probably won't laugh," I said, but really, what was there to laugh about? You had to have some nerve to burst out laughing when the person you love has just started talking about breaking up.

"Understood," Wada calmly agreed. There was no change in his expression.

And then he said something I absolutely did not see coming: "I'm thinking about writing a novel."

"A novel?" The word reverberated inside my head, but its meaning would not register. *A nah-vul . . .*

"Yeah. Does that sound weird?"

"Weird? No, but is that what you wanted to talk about? That's it?"

"That was it . . ."

I was ready to fall out of my chair. Wada could really be impossible to read sometimes. I was so exhausted by it all I ended up laughing.

"You laughed," Wada said, looking stricken.

I tried desperately to explain myself. "It's not that kind of laughter."

"Not that kind of laughter? What kind of laughter are we talking about here?" he asked earnestly. It was no use though. We were totally out of sync.

I drained my glass of water and sighed. That somehow managed to calm me down.

"You said this was going to be the bad kind of talk so I was nervous," I mumbled.

Wada looked back at me blankly.

"I didn't say it was bad. I only said it wasn't good."

"Which means it's going to be bad."

"Is that right? I'm sorry. I just meant it wasn't especially good news."

"Wada, you can be a tiny bit strange sometimes," I said sarcastically, trying to get him back for how nervous he'd made me.

"Really?" Wada folded his arms and pondered what I'd said.

We didn't seem to be getting anywhere this way, so I tried to go back to what he'd said a minute ago. "You're going to write a novel?"

"Yes," Wada said, finally coming back to what he was saying. "Actually, I started writing in high school and wrote for almost ten years. But not that long ago, I'd completely stopped writing. Then I got to know you, Takako, and all the people who come to the Morisaki Bookshop, and I felt inspired again. Now I feel this irresistible urge to write a novel that takes place at the bookshop. I'm not aiming to win any awards, of course, or trying to become a professional writer. I thought my drive to write was gone, but then I realized I still had it, and I just feel like it would be a shame to let it all end without really trying." He gave an embarrassed laugh.

Simple as I am, I completely forgot about what had happened a minute ago. What Wada said had moved me. It made me really happy that he'd opened up to me about what he'd been thinking about for some time on his own. Wada is always so earnest. Even if it wasn't a big deal to me, it's clear that he was really worried about revealing this. That alone made it important.

"I think it's a wonderful idea. I want to help."

"Really? I'm so glad to hear that. If it's okay, I'd like to do some research at the bookshop, to gather some ideas."

"Oh."

"Is there a problem?"

"My uncle Satoru and I are in the middle of a big fight at the moment."

"A fight with the owner? I'm kind of surprised that you got angry too."

Apparently, he hadn't noticed that I was a little angry with him a minute ago. But that wasn't the only problem. My uncle hadn't taken kindly to Wada, because he was my boyfriend. Right after we'd started going out, I'd brought him to the shop to introduce him to my aunt and uncle. My uncle completely ignored Wada, even when he greeted him. He stayed stock-still, acting like he was one of those see-no-evil monkey figurines.

"Do you think the owner dislikes me? Did I violate some book-shop protocol without realizing it?" Wada said, cocking his head to one side and furrowing his brow.

"No, not at all. That's just how he always is," I said, desperately trying to bluff my way through.

On our way home, Wada kept muttering to himself about how he'd always thought of my uncle as so bright and friendly.

Later, when I went to the bookshop alone and flew into a rage about my uncle's attitude, my uncle yelled, "He isn't the right kind of customer for the Morisaki Bookshop."

Beside him, Momoko shook her head in exasperation. "Come on, you just don't want him to steal away Takako."

"Don't talk nonsense. All I'm saying is that I can't stand these pseudo-intellectuals. Guys like that are inhuman brutes who think nothing of leaving girls in tears."

"Monsters?" I was beyond outraged now. I was dumbfounded.

"I'm worried he might make you cry. And why does he keep referring to me as the proprietor? It creeps me out. I can't stand it."

"You're unbelievable," Momoko said. "It's about time for you to move on and let Takako go. And Wada seems like a really great guy. He's tall and slender, and he's about a thousand times better looking than you."

"Under no circumstances will I allow him to enter the shop."

"Hmmm . . . You used to be so cool when you said, 'The shop is open to anyone and everyone,' but now it turns out that you want to choose the customers?" I said coldly.

My uncle seemed at a loss for words. Then he repeated the phrase he always said when he was stuck: "People are full of contradictions."

I was determined to help Wada write his novel no matter what. Wada seemed so happy when I offered. And when he was happy, I guess I was happy too.

"Please make up with the owner soon," Wada said as we waved goodbye at the turnstile in the train station. "Not because of my novel, of course. Just because."

————

The next day, on my way home from work, I stopped by the Morisaki Bookshop around closing time. I had come to make up with my uncle. It was a little annoying, but I didn't have a choice. Besides, Wada had asked me to. If I gave in, that would be the end of it.

When Momoko brought up the idea of my uncle not going on the trip, he really seemed deeply disappointed. He had to go for her sake too. So I decided to try changing my strategy.

"Hey, Uncle?"

"What?"

The storefront was already shuttered, so I stuck my head in the back entrance and called out to him. His voice sounded wary. At night, the damp smell inside the shop was even stronger.

"Come on, can't you let your guard down?" Forcing a smile, I tried to put him in a good mood by asking if he'd gotten any good books in lately. Whenever he gets talking about books, my uncle's bad mood vanishes right away. It's that simple. Soon he'd completely forgotten that we were fighting, and we were on our way.

"Oh, well, something came in yesterday that might be perfect for you."

"Really? What?"

"It's a classic that still hits home with readers today."

My uncle pulled Jun'ichirō Tanizaki's *In Praise of Shadows* from the stack and passed it to me.

"It's an essay, right? What does the title mean?"

"Hmmm . . . if I were to grossly oversimplify it, I'd say that it's about how we shouldn't just pay attention in our everyday lives to where the light is. We should look at the shadows as well. And behind that idea is a whole aesthetic sensibility. And I guess there's something about experiencing a Japanese sense of beauty. It all gets much, much deeper than that though. It might be a little difficult to read, but it's such a good book, you should give it a try."

"Thanks. I'll give myself plenty of time to read it."

"Give it a read now," he urged, briskly leaning in. It seemed like he wanted to sit next to me while I read the book so he could explain it. I recoiled, pulling away from my uncle.

"I'm okay right now. I'll read it carefully soon, someplace quiet and free from interruptions."

"How come? If you want to read it now, I can open up the store again."

"That's why I was saying I want to read it somewhere quiet."

"Where can you find a place quieter than here?"

Apparently, it never would have occurred to him that he was the one guilty of shattering the silence.

"So, about that trip," I said, returning the book to the shelf. My uncle's expression stiffened immediately, as if to say, *Here we go again*.

"It's okay if you just can't go," I said as a preamble, though I didn't believe that in the slightest. I lowered my gaze. "I feel like I always depend on you so much. I just wanted to do something to show my gratitude. So, I'm not asking you to do it if it's not possible, but Momoko wants to go, and it would be great if the two of you could go spend some time together." I said the lines I'd prepared in advance, putting as much emotion into it as I could.

"I want you to be able to keep the store open for a long, long time. And to do that, you have to remember to take time off. Otherwise, you're going to ruin your health. And if you died from working too much, I think my heart might burst."

Telling him all this was starting to make me uncomfortable. First of all, my uncle's the kind of person you couldn't kill if you tried. The idea of him overworking himself to death was too outlandish to believe. But he turned out to be ridiculously vulnerable to this approach. Sure enough, he was soon staring at me with tears in his eyes.

"Takako, you . . ."

"So, you understand what I mean?"

My uncle nodded several times, overcome with emotion. "Is that true? I really mean that much to you?"

"Well, that's why you should go," I said, losing no time.

"Ah, mmm-hmmm," my uncle replied automatically.

"And take good care of Momoko too. How about next week? I'm available then."

"What? Ahhhh." My uncle reluctantly agreed, although looking at the expression on his face, he didn't seem entirely convinced. My strategy had succeeded.

We left the shop and walked together to the station. The whole way, he kept mumbling, "Are you really sure you can run the store by yourself? I don't know."

I stood up straight and said, "Trust me," showing him how confident I was.

Once night fell, it turned thoroughly cold out. I wrapped my scarf tighter around my neck. My uncle was grumbling beside me, his breath making hazy white puffs that hung in the air for a moment and then vanished into the night.

7

The day of the trip, I woke in the morning and headed to the Morisaki Bookshop, bringing a bag with two days of clothes. My aunt and uncle were leaving straight from home, so I would be taking over for my uncle and running the bookshop right from the morning through the evening. Just thinking of it made my heart beat faster.

That may be one reason why I ended up leaving my place almost an hour early, which meant I ran right into the morning rush hour. I normally didn't have to be at work until ten, which meant I missed rush hour by a bit. So this was my first time back in those crowded trains since the days I was working at my old job. I ought to have mastered then how to fight my way onto a packed train, but it had been such a long time that I'd completely forgotten how to do it. As I steamed in the heat of the train, swaying to and fro in the throng of bodies, and got carried off by the current, I must've screamed to myself about thirty times.

Back when I used to spend every morning rocking back and forth in crowded trains, I encountered some strange people. People who muttered to themselves, or screamed in rage, people who threw themselves into you with clear malice. There was always some kind of trouble, and the whole train car would get drawn into it whenever someone was accused of groping or a fight broke out. Seeing something like that so early in the morning would leave me feeling profoundly exhausted. Now that I found myself back in a train car in that menacing environment for the first time in a while, that response didn't seem unreasonable. Being locked in with such misery every morning could definitely take a toll on your mind.

After enduring fifteen minutes in hell, I got off the train in Jimbocho and headed to the bookshop. It was still just a little after nine. The shop didn't open until ten so I was too early.

With nothing else to do, I went around inside cleaning every nook and cranny. I ended up becoming so focused on cleaning that before I knew it, it was time to open.

"All right, let's do this," I said, getting myself fired up as I raised the shutter and started my first day. Open up in the morning, tend the shop all day, and then at night, put the day's proceeds into the safe and lower the shutter. Of course, I wouldn't be able to give prices to any valuable books, so if customers came in wanting to sell them, I would tell them the situation and hold on to the books for them. As long as it was only for two or three days, I figured I ought to be able to do a decent job running the shop by myself.

Looking around the street, I saw that the other shops were preparing to open too. The heady scent of a sweet olive tree came drifting in from somewhere nearby. I made eye contact with Mr. Ijima, the owner of the closest bookshop, diagonally across the street, so I wished him good morning.

"Where's Satoru today?"

"He left on a trip."

"Oh my!" the owner said, his eyes wide with surprise. "That's pretty unusual. It's going to rain today, isn't it?"

"I'm so sorry about that," I said, apologizing for the weather in advance.

As usual, hardly any customers came by in the morning. That's how it always was, and I was used to it. I was content to sit back, relax, and wait for the customers to arrive. To be honest, I was happy just being surrounded by all the books, and I would've been content even if no one had come in.

Still, the fact that my uncle had already called three times that morning was more than I could take. It seemed like it made him terribly worried to be far away from the bookshop. I got tired of dealing with him, so I made an effort to reassure him and quickly hung up.

The time went by very slowly. I spent the period before noon dealing with the customers who trickled in, few and far between, dusting and organizing the books piled up along the wall, and stopping to flip through any that caught my eye.

I also picked up Jun'ichirō Tanizaki's *In Praise of Shadows* to give it a try since my uncle had been so enthusiastic about it. The book is a profound examination of the meaning of shadows, which emerges from Tanizaki's account of his own experiences. It's an argument to be skeptical about the brightness of Japan's cities. His writing was so powerful, I felt like he was right beside me, speaking to me. The book had such an irresistible pull that before I knew it, I was completely sucked in.

When the afternoon finally came, it actually did end up raining. At first it was only drizzling, but it became gradually more intense, and before I knew it, the whole of Sakura Street had turned black with rain.

In this neighborhood of used bookshops, there is no greater enemy than rain. It's a serious problem if the books get wet, plus the number of people coming in instantly drops. As I rushed outside to bring in the carts of books, I saw that in front of all the other bookshops on the street, people were racing to bring their merchandise inside too.

Even Mr. Ijima, who had been cracking jokes about it raining earlier, was now battling the rain.

We laughed bitterly as we both pulled our carts under the roof.

"It's really coming down," he said.

"It really is, isn't it?"

Massive clouds covered the sky, bringing stronger rain showers. Maybe it was a mistake after all to force my uncle to go on a trip. I hoped it wasn't raining over there. "Hmmm," I muttered to myself. "It looks like I won't have anything to do till the end of the day." I went back inside.

Once I pulled the door shut, the fierce sound of rain became a gentle whisper. The faint scent of the road wet with rain drifted into the shop, where it blended with the smell of old books.

The flow of customers came to a halt.

For a long moment, I sat in my usual spot behind the counter with my eyes closed. It was quiet, so very quiet. If I concentrated, I could make out faint sounds—the patter of raindrops hitting the window, the low hum of cars splashing through the rain. I had the peculiar feeling then that I had become one with the bookshop. I could feel my sense of self begin to dissolve and my consciousness expand.

No, no, I can't fall asleep, I thought. I'm the person they trusted to take care of the shop. No matter how much free time I have at the moment.

But being surrounded by books that had been around for so many years seemed to change the way I experienced the passing of time itself. I had a clear sense of myself as existing within it. If there are some professions that require stillness and others that call for action, running a secondhand bookshop falls into the first category. Of course, one can't just divide jobs into simple binaries like that. But it's true that the entire image one has in one's head of these bookshops comes down to a feeling of stillness and calm. I felt like I fit here perfectly, like I had come to rest in a spot that was just my shape and size. And I wanted to remain this way forever.

Had my uncle ever felt like this? The feeling must have been even more intense for him. The shop had been passed on to him from my grandfather and my great-grandfather. One of the reasons my uncle was proud of running the bookshop lay in the respect he held for those who had looked after it before him.

These were the thoughts that drifted through my head as I stared out a window misty from the rain.

After four o'clock, just as the rain lightened up, I suddenly heard the sound of the door clattering open.

"Hey, sorry to barge in."

It had been so long since I'd had a customer that I jumped off my stool. But when I realized it was Sabu, I sat back down, mumbling, "Ooh boy," just like my uncle. Apparently Sabu had come to check in on me just to kill time. His face bore a perfectly mischievous smile.

"How's it going today?" Sabu asked, sounding the way he always did when he asked my uncle that same question.

"It's not," I replied.

Sabu gave his usual giggle. The sound of his laughter reverberated inside the shop. Given how quiet it had been up until a moment ago, it all seemed a little strange to me. The atmosphere of the shop felt completely different when it was filled with the sound of people's voices. Which wasn't necessarily a bad thing.

"You're a curious person, aren't you?" he said. "You come every week to this shop that no one ever comes to."

"You're the curious one. You show up at this shop every day."

"Oh stop, you're embarrassing me."

"You mustn't be so modest."

"I give up. You win."

"Once again. And remember you said you didn't mind."

While we sipped our tea, we went back and forth like this, talking nonsense with a straight face. Sabu left without buying anything, as usual. Eventually the sun went down, and the rain, which had eased off, stopped completely. The clock on the wall marked off the minutes, and when I looked up, it was already seven o'clock—time to close. The day had seemed long, but it was over before I knew it. I slowly rose to my feet and prepared to close the shop.

At exactly that moment, my uncle called again, as if he'd timed it precisely. I told him that I'd closed the shop without any issues, and I asked him to please only call me once the next day.

"Okay, let's split the difference. Three times!" my uncle yelled over the phone. Good grief, what exactly were we splitting the difference of?

The room on the second floor was even more comfortable than before. Momoko, who had stayed here for a time, was now living with my uncle in Kunitachi, so no one was using it. Nevertheless, the room had been kept clean, and books were all neatly in order, probably thanks to Momoko. Pots of geraniums and gerbera daisies adorned the bay window, and there was a note Momoko had written, affixed to the window frame with instructions for watering them. I got the impression that if I forgot to water them somehow, it would be a major disaster. And there, nicely enshrined in the center of the room, was that well-used low dining table.

I opened the sliding door a bit to peek into the small connecting room and saw something frightening. In the dim light, I could see the room was packed tight with books from my uncle's collection. The dark silhouette of all those books, looming silently behind the door, was awfully creepy. I shut the door gently, pretending I hadn't seen anything.

Right at that moment, my cell phone started ringing on the dining table, and it startled me. When I looked at the screen, I saw the call was from Wada. I'd told him that today was going to be my first day tending the shop, so he was probably concerned about me.

"How'd it turn out?"

"Perfect. How about you? Things busy at work?"

"I've got my hands full."

"Take it easy. Sounds like you're too busy to write your novel."

"I'm taking my time, so it's not a problem. Hey, I should get back to work though."

"Okay. Don't work too hard. Thanks for calling. I know you're busy."

Afterward, I finished my simple dinner, took a shower, and then I was basically done with everything I needed to do. I lay on my futon, took a book from the shelves nearby, and flipped through it, but I was too sleepy to concentrate. Still, it seemed a shame to go to sleep like this. A tiny spider was crawling slowly across the ceiling above me. I followed him with my eyes for a while absent-mindedly.

Before long, I got up suddenly and opened the window. The chilly autumn wind rushed in. I could see the silver light of the moon shining in the sky in the distance. The noise and bustle of the neighborhood sounded far away. There was the low rumble of passing cars, the sound of people talking as they went down the street. Then came the sudden clatter of someone closing a shutter. After the sound faded, the silence deepened.

In Praise of Shadows.

I wasn't sure if this was the right situation for it, but I found myself murmuring those words. Then I turned off the lights in the room, sat by the window, and closed my eyes.

I had spent so many long nights this way. Back then, I couldn't conceive of the idea that that time in my life would ever end. But those days have passed. That period of my life has receded into the distance. There's no going back to the past. As I told myself this, I felt a sweet sorrow spread through my chest.

But there was no point in dwelling on that, I thought. I'm much happier now.

My life till this point had been simple, but that didn't mean it was trouble-free. I'd had my share of suffering and setbacks along the way. I sank to the bottom of a deep, dark sea, and for a time, I believed I didn't want to come back up. But on a quiet night like this, I could feel keenly how blessed I'd been, how all the wonderful people I have met along the way had lifted me up. I really had met some wonderful people. I opened my eyes a little and saw moonlight shining in through the window. Sitting in the gentle light, I could feel happiness slowly welling up within me.

Then, for some reason, memories from my childhood came back to me, one after another. It was like a door that had been closed had suddenly been thrown open.

In my own way, I was an unhappy child. Or rather, maybe I should say I was far more troubled in childhood than I was after I became an adult. I think it's partly because I was an only child and an introvert, and I didn't get to spend much time with my parents since they were both busy working. It's also because I wasn't able to properly deal with the anxiety and sadness I felt.

Since I couldn't talk to anyone about this, I couldn't find a way out of my problems, and little by little the sadness inside me grew until it felt like a massive balloon pressing down on me every night when I got into bed. Of course, it was always about childish things. They all seem trivial when I look back on them now. Like when I got depressed thinking about having to take a test in gym class right after summer break to see whether I could spin backward over the playground bars. Or when I heard a rumor that people buried dead bodies under cherry trees, and became afraid of the cherry tree in my backyard. Or when I became despondent after the boys in my class gave me the nickname "Bones" (because I was tall and kind of skinny).

There was nothing I looked forward to more in those days than going back to my grandfather's house every long vacation. My uncle Satoru would be there, waiting to see me. It was a huge help. For me, being with my uncle in his room was like a bulwark against the world. Once I'd made it there, I could relax. There was nothing more to worry about.

In his room, my uncle would listen sweetly as I rambled about all kinds of things. When I finally got tired of talking so much, he would pull out the right record from his collection, and the two of us would sing along at full volume. We were awfully noisy, and sometimes we would even get yelled at by my grandfather, who would come rushing up from the hall where all our relatives had gathered, his face bright red with rage. My uncle and I would put on meek expressions and pretend to be sorry, but as soon it was just the two of us, we would break out giggling. At school, I was always so timid, but with my uncle I felt so brave that it was like I wasn't my normal self.

The anxiety that I had trouble putting into words seemed to diminish a little bit. The rest of the world that up till then had seemed to be wasting away, now, with my uncle, was suddenly thrown open wide.

Looking back, I realized all of my memories of my uncle from that time made me feel like I was in some warm, sun-dappled spot. Was it nostalgia? Did I wish I could go back in time? I wasn't sure, but somehow I was on the verge of tears.

In that room lit only by moonlight, I revisited those sweet memories that had lain dormant behind a door within me, and it was like I was opening up one book after another, turning the pages until I finally fell asleep.

8

The next morning, the fair weather returned. Ragged clouds drifted across the clear autumn sky. The puddles glittered in the bright morning light.

"It's not going to rain today, right?" Mr. Ijima said from the other side of the street, not sounding all that confident.

"I don't think so, but . . ."

"If it does rain today, and I ever hear about Satoru going on a trip again, I'll use every ounce of strength in my body to stop him," Mr. Ijima said as he went back to getting ready to open. I couldn't tell whether or not he was joking.

Fortunately, however, the sky kept my fears at bay. Thanks to which, business was much better than the day before. From the morning, there was a steady drip of customers coming and going. I even sold a Hideo Kobayashi volume with a price tag of five thousand yen.

Then, sometime before noon, I had an unusual visit from a pair of girls who looked like college students. They both vaguely resembled each other, but the one in the flowery dress had an expensive-looking single-reflex camera hanging from her neck. They each carefully examined a single book, then asked me if I could recommend anything. After a great deal of thought, I suggested Tōson Shimazaki's *Before the Dawn*. It seemed to interest them and they bought it.

As they were leaving, the girl with the camera said in a polite tone of voice, "Would you mind if I took a photograph?"

"Oh, not at all," I said. The girl's eyes lit up, and she immediately started taking pictures of the shop.

"Um, can I take one of you as well?"

I reluctantly sat down in the chair behind the counter.

Perhaps because I had too stern a look on my face, she said timidly, "And, um, could I ask you to just look the way you usually do?" But there was no way I could do that in front of the camera. For the most part, when I have time to myself at the shop, I sit there with a dazed look on my face. Getting my picture taken like that would just mean making a fool of myself. In the end, I made up some excuse and stepped back, and basically fled to a corner of the shop.

"To tell the truth, I've liked the feel of this store for a while, and I've been wanting to photograph it," the girl told me as she clicked away at the shutter. The girl who came with her stood smiling beside her. They were cute and they seemed really nice.

"Wow. Is that right?"

"It's got a style to it. And the atmosphere inside is really wonderful."

"I guess you're right," I said nonchalantly. I guess you could say that there's something special about the atmosphere inside an old wooden building. Though my original impression the first time I came here was simply that it was falling apart.

"But, there's always, kind of . . ."

"A weird old guy who's hard to talk to?" I said with a wicked grin.

The girl seemed flustered. "Oh no, not, I mean . . . well, yeah, actually."

"I'm not surprised."

I laughed out loud, ignoring the blank looks on their faces.

"You've been incredibly helpful. Thank you so much. We'll be sure to read the book too."

After the girl had finished shooting, she thanked me politely, and the two of them left the shop.

Things like that kept me pretty busy, and before I knew it, it was nighttime. After I checked the ledger and put the day's take in the safe, I finished a simple cleanup and closed the shop. And in a complete change from yesterday, for some reason my uncle never even called once that day. Had he finally started to trust me? I couldn't help feeling something was missing. In the end, I finished preparing to close, then went out so I could buy ingredients for dinner.

That night, Tomo was coming over. When I'd told her that I'd be staying at the shop again after such a long time, she said she just had to come by after work. Back when I lived at the shop, she came to see me many times and had fallen in love with the place.

Since she was coming over around nine, I used the time until then to prepare a dinner that I'd learned from Momoko when she lived here. Momoko still made lunch for my uncle, which meant that there was already rice and seasonings there.

It was a menu of pure Japanese food, passed on directly from Momoko: stewed chicken and hijiki seaweed, fried tofu, salt-broiled mackerel pike, miso soup with deep-fried tofu and turnip slices, and rice with red shiso. There was only one gas burner, so cooking took more time than expected. I was impressed that Momoko was able to make such delicious food every night with a setup like this.

At exactly nine, I heard a cheerful voice call out "Good evening" from the back door, and I went downstairs to welcome Tomo.

"Ooh, something smells good."

"I've just been cooking. You haven't eaten yet, have you? I thought we could eat together."

"I wouldn't want to impose . . ."

"Not at all. I have to eat anyway."

Tomo and I first got to know each other and became close back when she was working part time as a waitress at the Saveur. The first time I met her I had a sense right away that we could be friends. When I told her that later on, to my delight she said she'd felt the same way at the time. Since then, we've developed one of those rare friendships that are hard to come by. There was something in the way she talked that felt calm and reserved. Her black hair was shiny and her skin was pale white. If you looked up the entry for a traditional Japanese beauty in the dictionary, the picture would look something like Tomo. And moreover, she was talented. She had studied Japanese literature in graduate school. I'd heard she was working now as a librarian at some college. Today, she was wearing a stylish black dress and a silver necklace with a bird motif. It struck me that she seemed to have an innate sense of what clothes suited her best.

With Tomo's help, I spread out all the dishes I'd prepared on the low dining table. It was quite cramped with the two of us eating there, but it was the best we could do.

After Tomo sat down in front of the dining table, she looked around the room. "Ah, it's been a long time since we've been here together," she said emphatically. "It's such a relaxing spot, isn't it?" She was quick to notice the book I'd left on the windowsill, Hyakken Uchida's *Train of Fools*, which I'd started to read the night before after getting into my futon, hoping to feel like I was going on a trip too.

"Oh, I've read this too," she said, her eyes sparkling.

Train of Fools is a travel diary written in the 1950s. In the book, the writer sets out on a trip, with no particular purpose and no particular destination in mind. He just somehow finds himself leaving on a trip. And so the trip becomes an end in itself. There's something funny about this man, who's already past sixty, earnestly committing himself to carrying out a plan that simply popped into his head one day, though strictly speaking, the plan is both meaningless and pointless. There's a richness to the writing; the sentences flow like water. Reading them, you get to savor the feeling of traveling, and as a bonus you get a glimpse of the customs and culture of the era.

"Hyakken Sensei is wonderful, isn't he?" Tomo said with a smile.

I could tell how deeply she loved his writing by the way she'd automatically called him Sensei.

"He's the best. And his companion, Himalayas. They're too adorable together."

"I wanted to be on the trip with them."

"They're so hard to please though. Don't you think if you actually went it would be a disaster?"

"But they're so cute—and they seem like pretty cheerful old guys," Tomo said with a sweet smile. There was something so maternal in that smile that it startled me.

Tomo chewed her food slowly as she ate. For some reason, I always tended to rush impatiently through the meal, so this time I followed her example and ate slowly. She said she hadn't eaten Japanese food in a while. She tended to prefer spicy food. She'd always been a light eater, and since she'd been busy at work she'd gotten in the habit of eating whatever she could throw together. Seeing her across from me breaking out into a smile and telling me how delicious it was, I couldn't stop myself smiling in return.

We talked about a lot of things over dinner—about our jobs, about the books we'd read recently. We were always emailing and calling each other on the phone, but it was a joy to talk face-to-face like this. Even after the meal was over, we stayed at the table talking.

"But being a librarian is perfect for you."

"A college library's nice, but my real dream was to work at the National Library."

"Oh, that's the library that has every book that's been published?"

"Exactly. But I flunked the exam for the job."

"Really? What a shame."

"The place I work now might not be big, but the library does have a collection of old and important texts. I get a thrill out of it. Still, sometimes the youthful exuberance of all those college students can get a bit overwhelming," Tomo said. Her voice had a gentleness and a maturity about it. Even the way she used chopsticks was elegant— all that remained of her mackerel pike was the head and the bones. There was nothing to praise about what I'd left on my plate. She must have been raised well, I said to myself. In fact, I'd heard that Tomo's family ran the biggest construction company in the area. Basically, she was the boss's daughter. "It's not as nice as it sounds," she insisted.

"What do you mean 'youthful exuberance'? There's hardly any age difference between you and them."

"I guess I'm no longer that exuberant."

"Haven't you found any college guys you connect with?"

With a girl like Tomo at the library reception desk, there were probably lots of students who were crazy about her. I let myself imagine some male student who saw Tomo in the distance and fell madly in love. But Tomo quickly dispelled my delusions.

"No, not at all. But what about you? Are things going well with Wada?"

"Um, yeah, I guess," I said, flustered to find myself the focus of the conversation.

Right at that moment, my phone chimed like I'd timed it perfectly. I looked and saw it was a text from Wada. Would I mind if he visited me at the shop for a little bit? He was about to call it a day and leave the office.

"Wada says he wants to come over. Is that okay?"

"Absolutely, sure. I want to meet him."

I'd talked to Tomo a lot about Wada, but the two had never met. So, it seemed like a good opportunity. Let's invite him over. Although the room was too small for three people.

Tomo's here, I said, but come over.

Less than ten minutes later, we heard a voice shout "Hey!" from outside the window.

"Welcome," I said to Wada, who had just made it up the stairs and come into view.

"Good evening. It's a pleasure to meet you," Tomo said, with a huge smile on her face.

"Oh, Miss, um, Ms. Tomo, I've heard so much about you. It's a pleasure to meet you as well." Wada bowed quickly to Tomo.

"You don't need to call her 'Miss,'" I said laughing, but in response to Wada's earnestness, Tomo straightened her posture and bowed in return.

"No, the pleasure is all mine."

"Wada, you already had dinner, right? I'm sorry. We ate everything. If I'd known you were coming, I would've prepared a plate for you."

"No, don't worry about it. I'm heading home in a bit."

Wada seemed restless for some reason. He was sitting there in a formal posture in one corner of the room. When I asked him why, he said he was just excited because it was his first time coming to the second-floor room.

"But it seems wrong to barge in and have a look around without the owner's permission."

It seemed like he was trying desperately to suppress his urge to lick every surface in the room.

"You say that, but then you came over anyway, didn't you?" I said, astounded.

"I let my curiosity get the better of me. But I was wrong to cross that final line. One mustn't give in to passion at the cost of courtesy. Moreover, there's a high likelihood that Mr. Morisaki hates me." There was a look of anguish on Wada's face now, but he hadn't budged from his stiff, formal posture.

"You're just as funny as Takako said you were."

"Right?"

We nodded our heads in agreement as we struggled desperately to keep from laughing.

"What? What's funny about me?" Wada asked earnestly, in another display of how serious he was by nature.

We couldn't take it anymore, and the two of us finally burst out laughing.

It was a lively night, a complete change from the night before.

When it was nearly time for the last train of the night, Tomo had to leave, and Wada decided to leave with her. I wanted to get a little air too, so I went with them part of the way.

After we said goodbye to Tomo at the entrance to the subway, I immediately turned to Wada and asked him what his impression of her was. "Tomo's wonderful, isn't she?"

"Oh, sure she is."

Deep down, I had been nervous about how Wada would respond to meeting Tomo, but mostly he just seemed indifferent. On the one hand, I was relieved, but I was also disappointed that he hadn't quite seen how wonderful she was. I was proud to call her my friend. Why couldn't he see how charming she was? It irritated me.

Wada, however, kept talking and looking rather confused. "It's just that she . . ."

"What?"

"I don't know. It's just a feeling, but it's like she's there, but she's not really there."

"Huh?"

"I don't know what to make of it. Maybe she's the kind of person who's used to being alone. Or rather, it's like she's the kind who prefers to remain alone."

"You think so? I don't get that sense from her at all."

What Wada had said was so unexpected, I could hardly grasp it.

I'd always thought that Tomo was the kind of cheerful girl that anyone would love.

"I don't know. Maybe it's her way of protecting herself. I'm not sure how to describe it. It might be because I can be like that myself that I was able to pick up on it. It's like the moment we laid eyes on each other, I had a sense she and I were the same type of person. I don't know. It's probably just that she was nervous meeting me for the first time. Sorry. Forget I said anything."

As I listened to him, I was less concerned about Tomo and more concerned about Wada.

What he was saying at that moment . . . I'd secretly sensed that he hadn't completely opened his heart to me. I realized I was right, and it made me feel lonely.

Wada stopped ahead of the traffic signal on the avenue and said, "This is far enough. I can walk back from here by myself."

"Or you could spend the night at the shop?" I asked, pretending I was joking.

"I couldn't. That's the owner's . . ."

"That's okay. I understand," I said, cutting him off.

His answer was so obvious, I couldn't even be disappointed. But the fact that the answer was obvious made me a little sad.

"Good night."

To hide what I was feeling from Wada, I turned on my heels and ran back to the shop without waiting for his response.

The next day, I was in a dark mood right from the morning.

I sat in my chair, staring blankly, lost in thought. Ever since I'd gotten to know Wada, my brain had been split in two, with the affirmative side of me and the negative side perpetually locked in debate. This morning that debate reached a boiling point.

I'd find myself reacting to every little thing he did or said, trying to gauge the depth of his love, and I'd think, What an annoying, clingy person. And yet the moment I fell in love, wasn't that what I became?

On this point, my affirmative side tried to convince my negative side, *This shows how much you love him*, to which, my negative side promptly answered back, *This is further proof of what an annoying person you can be*. Today, once again, my affirmative side had the weaker position, and my negative side was in top form.

"Um . . ."

I was suddenly startled to realize someone was speaking to me.

I looked up, feeling flustered, and saw that Takano was almost hiding behind one of the bookshelves, looking my way.

"Wait, Takano, how long have you been here?"

"I just came in."

Checking my watch, I saw it was almost noon. He must have come by on his break from the coffee shop. Takano was wearing only a T-shirt with three-quarter-length sleeves and a character printed on it who looked like a disintegrating Mickey Mouse. For some reason, he dressed lightly even in the cold months. Probably because in his heart he was still a boy.

"Say something when you come in. Or just don't come in so quietly."

"I'm sorry. I did say something, but you had this look on your face like you were deep in thought." Takano was scratching his head, like he couldn't figure out why I was mad at him. I was embarrassed because I realized that I was taking my frustrations out on him.

After I cleared my throat and regained my composure, I asked, "Is there anything you need?"

"I heard from my boss that you've been running the store since the day before yesterday."

"That is correct."

"So, um, there was something I wanted to talk to you about."

"That's why I was asking. What is it?"

"Well, it has to do with Tomoko Aihara."

"Tomo?"

Was this déjà vu? We had definitely been in this exact same situation before. I was alone in the shop, Takano came in, mentioned Tomo . . .

That's right. Takano was in love with Tomo. Intensely so. Back then, Takano had asked me to act as a go-between since I was good friends with Tomo. But just as they were becoming close, Tomo quit her part-time job at the coffee shop to find a real job, and after that, there were no more signs of progress in their relationship.

I sat there at the counter with my head resting in my hand. "Really? What is it now?" I said, totally indifferently. To be honest, my brain was already at capacity thinking about my own situation. I didn't have any interest in what Takano had to say.

"Could you please not sound so obviously annoyed?" Takano said, like he was losing his nerve. "You don't know what it's like. Your life is one happy day after another."

"Wait a second. You came to the shop to tell me something. Don't just sit there and sulk."

"I can't help but sulk after what happened," Takano said and laughed a little at himself. What a gloomy guy, I thought. He was sulking in such a terrible way that I found myself recoiling a little. It was probably safer not to tell him that Tomo had come over the night before.

"But can I tell you something?" Takano let out a sad sigh after he asked the question. Then he started to tell me this story.

Even after Tomo quit working at the coffee shop, they kept texting each other (mostly about books). Still, Takano was always the one who texted her first, so to avoid bothering her, he made sure to let enough time go by between texts. But about two months ago, he sent her a text for the first time in a while, and not only did he not get a reply, the text itself never even arrived. After that, he tried texting her dozens of times, but he always got an error message in return, and they never reached her.

"Which means she must've blocked my number? I mean otherwise my texts should get through, right?"

I couldn't believe Tomo would do something like that. Supposing she had, did that mean that Takano had done something truly terrible? As a test, I tried sending her a text right then: Thanks for coming last night. See you soon.

As expected, a "transmission complete" message appeared on the screen of my phone. I held up my phone to Takano, who stared at it like he was about to devour it with his eyes. He was silent for a moment, and then he looked up at the ceiling and yelled, "Why!?!?"

"Takano, do you have any recollection of, say, standing watch outside her home, or maybe sifting through her trash, or, I don't know, bugging her room?"

I'd heard a lot of stories about people who were driven to act like that under the strain of a love they could never share with the object of their affection. But Takano turned all red and denied everything.

"What makes you think I could have anything to do with a crime

like that? My boss is always saying that I have trouble reading between the lines, but I would never do something so awful to Tomo,
let alone anything like stalking."

"You're right. I'm sorry. It's so odd for her to do something like
that, that I had to check. There's no way a timid guy like you would
pull a stunt like that."

"Exactly!" Takano said, standing up a little straighter.

It was at that moment that Tomo's quick reply came back. It
must have been her lunch break. The text said, I want to thank you
for dinner last night. Come over to my place next time.

Delighted, I replied, How about next week?

Takano watched me with a look of despair in his eyes.

"Why? But why? Why only you?" he whined. There was an ur-
gency in his voice. But no matter how many times he asked me, I
didn't have any answer for him. Still, as I remembered how pretty
Tomo had looked last night, I felt sympathy for Takano. If I were
a man, I'd probably fall in love with Tomo too. And if one day she
blocked my number, I'd probably spend a week in bed. Yesterday, I
could only think about my relationship with Wada, but now, listening to Takano talk, I was fixated again on what Wada had said
about her.

"Well, Takano, what are you going to do?"

"I'm going to look for a book."

"Heh?"

It was such a random, off-the-wall response that I practically
screamed at him. How could looking for a book have anything
to do with what was going on with Tomo? "There's a book that
Tomoko wants. It was a really long time ago, but she was talking to
the owner at the Saveur, and she told him that there's a book she'd
always wanted to get, but she'd never been able to find it. I was, um,
listening nearby."

"What book?"

"I think the title is *The Golden Dream*. I've forgotten the name of the author, but it sounded like an old Japanese text, I think, probably a novel."

"So your plan is to find that book and give it to her as a present?"

"The fourteenth of next month is her birthday, right? If possible, I'd like to give it to her then. I don't know that much about books like that, but I was thinking that you might know more."

Despite what Takano had said, I'd never once seen a book with that title in the shop.

"Well, let's suppose you give her the book, what would you want her to do?"

"I don't want anything in exchange. It's only for my own satisfaction. I'm not trying to get her attention or win her over or anything. If she's avoiding me, then we can pretend it's from you."

What Takano said seemed laudable to me. I could tell from the tone of his voice that he truly was thinking of Tomo. He reminded me of that song I learned in grade school, "Donna Donna," about a calf being carted away from its mother. I'm sure the look in Takano's eyes at that moment was the same as the calf "with a mournful eye" in the lyrics.

"Tomoko probably just thinks of me as some guy she used to work with at her old part-time job, but to me, her smile is the reason I never quit the coffee shop. It's what made me able to go on working. So I want to find a way to express my gratitude for those years. I'll be satisfied as long as it makes her happy."

"Okay, I understand." After hearing what he felt, there was no way I could refuse to help him. "In that case, I'll help you look for the book. With the two of us, it shouldn't be any trouble. I want to make Tomo happy too."

"Thank you so much." And with that Takano's expression finally brightened a tiny bit.

———

That night, my aunt and uncle stopped by to check on things a little before I closed the shop. It would've been better for them to have gone straight to their home in Kunitachi, but my uncle couldn't help himself. I proudly informed him that there had been absolutely no problems at the shop. Thanks to the effects of the hot spring, Momoko's skin was even more lustrous than usual. "It was really fun," she said as she handed me a gift box of hot spring steamed buns. My uncle, however, was standing nearby, looking gloomy.

"That reminds me. You stopped calling after the second day," I said.

My uncle just mumbled "Yeah" in response. He looked a little unwell.

I was worried and looked to Momoko, who tried to explain. "It's been so long since we've been on a trip. I think we're a little bit tired. Don't worry about him. He really enjoyed it."

"Hmmm . . . really?" I thought it was a little odd, but I didn't pursue the matter any further. If they both said they'd enjoyed themselves, then that was enough for me.

"Well, I can close up. Leave the rest to me."

I wanted to fulfill my responsibilities right up to the end, so I had them go home first.

I had to work the next day too. My days at the Morisaki Bookshop had come to an end. I wanted to go on living at the shop, but instead I closed the shutter tightly and went back to my home and my normal life.

9

The following week, the cold air retreated and the warm days returned for a time. At midday, it felt hot wearing a jacket.

I tried to find the book that Tomo wanted, *The Golden Dream*, just as I had promised Takano.

I asked my uncle about it first, since that seemed the surest way to find any book.

But my uncle said he'd never seen or even heard of the book. I'd taken it for granted that he, of all people, would know it if it was an old Japanese book, but my assumption was totally wrong. And to make things worse, he barely showed any interest, which was so unlike him. Normally, my uncle would've gotten all worked up, searched until he found it. Lately, my uncle had seemed odd (he was odd before, of course, but not in this way). It was like he was profoundly tired. When I got worried and asked him if he was all right, he turned it around and asked me what I was talking about, so I figured there wasn't much to worry about.

With no other options, I made the rounds of the secondhand bookshops on the way home from work, keeping up my search for the book. Takano had assumed it was some kind of novel, but if my uncle didn't know it there was a decent chance that was wrong too, so I even popped into some shops that specialized in illustrated books.

In a mountain of thousands of old books, I was searching for a single volume, with only the slightest clue to go on. I found it surprisingly fun—like a treasure hunt. I wanted to find it for Takano, but I had also become deeply curious about the book itself. What kind of a book would Tomo want so badly? Was it funny? Maybe it was the kind of book that could change your whole perspective on life? I'd been feeling uneasy about things with Wada since last week, which only made me want a book like that even more. But the search proved to be more arduous than expected. As I made the rounds, not only could I not find the book, I couldn't even find a person who knew of its existence. And when I asked, Wada said he didn't know it either. It seemed the book that Tomo wanted to find was only for the true diehards.

But the harder it was to find the book, the more my interest in it grew.

My next step was to ask my uncle to get me into the auction being held at the Rare Book Hall in Jimbocho.

When you run a secondhand bookshop, the auction is your best opportunity to acquire books in large quantities. You could even say that it's nearly impossible to keep a bookshop going if you don't attend the auctions regularly. So, of course, all the bookshop owners of Jimbocho would be at the auction in the Rare Book Hall. It was easy to gather information there, and you could find a rare book without having to walk to all the shops.

To be honest though, the auctions were not exactly my cup of tea. While it was a relatively friendly scene because I knew so many people, there was a solemnity in the air that I found stressful.

I knew I would be out of place once the auction began in earnest. So, during the initial open period, meant to allow people to check out the items on auction, I stayed at my uncle's side and looked around for the book. This was the only occasion when my uncle seemed to concentrate, taking notes as he looked over the items. It didn't seem right to get in his way, so I kept my mouth shut and studied all the titles of the books in front of me. In the end, I didn't find what I was looking for. When I asked the bookshop owners I knew, they all said they'd never heard of the book.

I snuck out of the venue and stood in the hallway, grumbling to myself. If I couldn't find the book in this neighborhood after this much searching, where on earth would I ever find it? Of course, it was conceivable I'd missed it, but Takano had been checking the shops diligently too, and had been searching for more information online. But for all that, he hadn't turned up anything worthwhile.

Talking it over with Takano at the Saveur, we came to the conclusion that our best bet was to try the Book Festival.

Held from the end of October to the beginning of November, the Book Festival was Jimbocho's biggest event of the year.

For this week alone, this neighborhood, where time always seemed to go by so peacefully, was completely transformed. Carts of used books and rows of bookshelves lined the streets, and they even set out stands selling yakisoba and candy-covered fruit. Lots of people came, all looking for books. Once this time of year came around, I couldn't help but feel excited. It made me happy to see that so many people loved books. It often seemed as if only a limited number of people thought of Jimbocho as a crucial part of their lives, but in fact, there were all these people who loved it. I admit I found it all deeply moving.

Naturally, the Morisaki Bookshop was part of the festival every year. As a small shop, we did things differently from the bigger stores on the avenue. My uncle would run a sale on the books on the carts that fit snugly in front of the shop, and he set up a bargain corner inside. This year, Momoko had taken care of all the preparations, so there didn't seem to be much I could do to help. My uncle, who loved a good festival, was in such a frenzy this time of year that he could barely think about business, but this time he said, "Trust me, I've got it all under control."

Because of work I was only able to go to the festival for a single day. On that day alone, I was able to do my part, helping out at the shop from the morning on. Inside, we could hear the lively music coming from the main avenue, where the event booths were set up. From the other direction, the smell of sweet sauces and the aroma of grilled meat drifted to us on the breeze from Sakura Street, where the food stands were lined up.

At lunch, the three of us stood out front eating okonomiyaki and sausages my uncle had bought at the food stands. "This is so good," my uncle said, in ecstasy.

"This kind of food is more about the feeling," Momoko remarked coolly. "The taste is really nothing special."

Later on, after the sun had gone down, I joined Takano, who was now finished with work, and we wandered around searching for *The Golden Dream*. We hurried through the throngs of people, checking literally all the shops from one end of the street to the other. As Takano walked beside me, he turned and mumbled sadly, "When we did this three years ago, Tomoko was with us."

It was true: Tomo had been with us then. And now she had blocked his number. I guess you could say that for Takano that day was *The Golden Dream* itself.

Given the limited time and the large number of shops, it didn't seem possible to go to all of them, so we decided midway to divide them between us and meet up again in front of the Morisaki Bookshop in an hour. In the end, my search was fruitless. Takano's too. As soon as I saw the look on his face, I knew there was no point in even asking.

That evening, after the festival had come to an end, Takano and I went out for curry with my aunt and uncle.

"So, you couldn't find it. I guess that's how it goes," Momoko said as she devoured her beef curry, ignoring the fact that Takano didn't seem to have an appetite.

"It's not a book I know. I apologize I couldn't be more helpful," my uncle said, feeling sorry for Takano. My uncle, of course, had ordered his curry mild.

"There's no need to apologize," Takano said. He was shaking his head briskly, yet it was obvious from the way he let his shoulders droop that he was heartbroken.

I was exhausted, and I was beginning to wonder if there was any point in continuing our search. Wouldn't it be better to ask Tomo instead, rather than taking such a roundabout way? We had no definite proof that Tomo didn't already have the book to begin with. But Takano had done his best, even if it was in vain. And that was one of his finer qualities, so I decided not to push him any further.

"It's a shame we didn't find it, but the fact that you looked for it will make Tomo happy."

"That's right. It's what you did that matters."

"You think so?"

"Besides, you can't expect to seduce a girl with a single book," Momoko said.

Takano leaned across the table and protested frantically. "That wasn't my intention at all. Seduce her? The thought never even crossed my mind."

"Oh, is that right?"

"It is," I said, coming to Takano's defense. "Besides, Takano's texts are getting blocked. Let's not get ahead of ourselves."

"You mean she dislikes you that much? That's tragic," Momoko said, turning her face to the heavens dramatically. What she said sounded like a death sentence to Takano.

"Hey, that's enough out of you," my uncle scolded.

"Takako . . ." For some reason, Takano was looking at me bitterly.

"Oh, sorry, that was thoughtless of me," I said and immediately covered my mouth with both hands. But it was too late. The part about his number being blocked was supposed to be a secret.

"You've got to be careful about this one. She has a pretty big mouth," Momoko said.

"Nah," my uncle said. "Takako's tight-lipped about secrets, just like she's tight about money."

Takano turned to me and bowed his head, ignoring the nonsense coming from my aunt and uncle. "Anyway, I apologize for bringing you into this, Takako."

"I told you there's nothing to apologize for. I enjoyed it. It was fun looking around."

"I'm happy to hear that, but I still owe you an apology."

"I just told you that you really don't. But if Tomo is okay with it, I'll see if I can invite you to her birthday party," I said.

Despite how dejected he felt, Takano was sweet to be so considerate. That's the kind of person he was. And I believe that's why the people around him all loved him. In my heart, I thought, wouldn't it be nice if we brought Tomo and him together for a bit . . .

That Sunday, I paid a visit to Tomo's home in Nezu. It was my first time there. She didn't work on the weekend, so I stopped by on my way home from the office. Her apartment was less than five minutes from the train station, a corner unit on the second floor of a two-story building only for women. I pressed the intercom button, holding the cake I'd bought as a gift at a shop near the station. Tomo came out right away with a smile on her face and welcomed me in.

Tomo's apartment was not all that different from what I had imagined: simple, clean, and stylish. The warm-toned curtains, furniture, and bedspread were all color-coordinated. It was the apartment of a young woman of refined taste. Except for one thing: the bookshelves were enormous. They went all the way up to the ceiling. I had the urge to ask if she had ordered them from a trade supplier. Of course, they were tightly packed with books with no space left to spare. It looked like she was ready to open her own little bookshop. When you visit a friend's place, it's normal to take an interest in the contents of their bookshelves. While Tomo made us tea, I took the liberty of thoroughly examining the contents of those enormous bookshelves. It was mostly old Japanese novels, but there were also books by foreign writers like Baudelaire and Rodenbach, and fantasy series like The Lord of the Rings and The Earthsea Cycle. (As far I could tell, the book Takano and I had been looking for wasn't there.)

"It seems like it must've been hard to move in," I said, looking over the bookshelves.

Tomo understood what I meant. "Oh, absolutely!" she said. "These books alone filled ten cardboard boxes. I'm trying not to get any more books now. But what do you do, Takako, to organize your books or pack them up when you move?"

"I don't have that many books yet. I don't worry much about holding on to them, so I tend to gather them up and sell them."

"I see." Tomo fell quiet. "I'd better start selling more, or I'll be in trouble. But once I like a book, I just can't let go of it."

After tea, while we ate the elaborate Southeast Asian dinner that Tomo had prepared, I said that since her twenty-sixth birthday was coming up so soon, we should go out to dinner again to celebrate. Surprisingly she had almost nothing planned for her birthday, so it came together quite quickly.

"I wonder if we should invite Takano," I asked, trying to take advantage of this moment in the conversation.

At the sound of his name, Tomo, who was reaching with her chopsticks to pick up a fresh spring roll, suddenly froze. She turned and looked at me with a pained expression on her face. "Did you say Takano?"

"Yeah, is that a bad idea?"

"It's not a bad idea, it's just . . ." Tomo said hesitantly. I could tell by the tone of her voice how troubled she was, and I hesitated to go any further. The situation might be more serious than I'd thought. But for Takano's sake, I wanted to find out what he'd done wrong. Speaking quickly, I told her what I'd heard from Takano and politely asked if something had happened.

"But look," Tomo said, hesitating even more. "I'd quit my job at the coffee shop, and I didn't expect we'd be in touch after that."

It was hard to believe Tomo would block his number for such a trivial reason. She and Takano had gotten along so well that I thought it might develop into a romantic relationship. Unless Takano had committed some unpardonable mistake, there was no way to explain it.

"Did he, by any chance, do something that upset you?"

"Absolutely not," Tomo said, looking up in surprise. That was the one thing she flatly denied. And I was relieved to hear it. At some point, I had started feeling like Takano's mother.

"Nothing like that happened. Takano is really purehearted. I admire that. There's nothing wrong with him. There's something wrong with me," Tomo said. She cast her gaze downward, pursing her lips so tightly they formed a straight line. I saw tears welling up in her eyes, and I felt myself trembling all over.

"That's not true, Tomo. There's nothing wrong with you. It's not your fault if you don't feel the same as Takano."

I realized I'd let slip something I shouldn't have. Takano had never said a word to her about how he loved her.

"I'm sorry, I, um . . ."

"It's okay. I was well aware of the fact that he cared for me. I sensed it somehow that day the three of us went to the Book Festival such a long time ago. But even though I knew, I always pretended not to notice. I took advantage of the fact that Takano never said anything, and I feigned ignorance, so we stayed friends."

"That's why I don't think you did anything wrong."

"That's not true. There's something wrong with me. The moment I receive that kind of attention from a member of the opposite sex, I suddenly become frightened, and I try to close myself off. I'm frightened that if I reciprocate I won't be able to handle it. I know it's crazy, but I can't help it."

Tomo no longer paid any attention to the food on the table. She fell silent and just kept looking down. The tears that had been welling up in her eyes now seemed about to fall. I felt as if I had accidentally driven her to this point. My chest hurt just looking at her. The room became so silent we could hear the faint buzz of the fluorescent light on the ceiling.

I was unsure whether I could ask anything more. Perhaps sensing this, Tomo said, "Can we talk just a little bit more? I'm not sure I can put it into words well, but I want to tell you."

"Shall I make us some tea?" I said cheerfully, in an effort to keep her from getting more depressed. "You'll feel a little better with something warm to drink."

"Oh, I . . ."

Tomo started to get up, but I stopped her and went into the kitchen, where I quickly cleaned the teapot and cups we'd just used, and made us a fresh pot of black tea.

"Thank you," Tomo said, accepting her cup, and she slowly brought it to her lips. "There's nothing wrong with Takano. There's something wrong with me." She repeated the same words she'd said a moment ago, sounding a little calmer. "I told you before about how I started reading."

"Um, yeah, you said it was your sister's influence."

"That's right. I had a sister who was five years older. From when I was little, all I did was imitate her, not just with books, with everything. Unlike me, my sister was smart and beautiful. She was the kind of person who could do anything. She had a little bit of a wild temper, but she was always kind to me." Tomo closed her eyes for a moment, as if she were recalling her memories of that time in her life. Then she started to speak again. "My sister had a boyfriend she went out with from when they were in high school. He was a very quiet person, the opposite of my sister. To tell the truth, it was because of his influence that my sister started to read books. And then I let myself be influenced so much that I started to love him the way she did. He was my first love. Still, I was in grade school, and I didn't recognize it. I just played with them a lot. I was in middle school when I became aware of it. But anyone could see how well suited they were for each other, and for a long time I never even considered uttering a word about what I felt. I was happy enough that they were there, and that sometimes they would let me into their little world."

Tomo took a sip of tea and glanced at me, as if to check my reaction. I nodded silently, as if to say, *I'm listening*, and she smiled sadly in response.

"Right after I turned seventeen, my sister died in an accident. The driver of the bus she always took to the university fell asleep and collided head-on with an oncoming car."

Tomo pursed her lips and closed her eyes, like she was mourning the death of her sister. I started to say something, but she shook her head and cut me off. "When my sister died, I was so sad that I thought I would die too. It really felt like my chest would burst. But after a while, I noticed that somewhere in my heart I was feeling another emotion. It was hope, hope that after what happened, he might turn his attention to me. It was such an ugly, ugly, sinister feeling."

"But Tomo . . ."

Tomo was still looking down, her gaze fixed to a point on the floor. Like she was staring into a vast, black ocean beneath her. No matter how many times I turned it over in my mind, I couldn't find the right words to say, something that might weaken the hold this had over her.

"I couldn't forgive myself for feeling that way. Nothing anyone tried to tell me could change that. That in the midst of all the sadness I felt after losing the sister I loved so much, I could still . . ." At that point, Tomo abruptly stopped talking and looked up. "I'm sorry. It's such a depressing story," she said apologetically.

I kept shaking my head. "And your sister's boyfriend, how did he . . ."

"I haven't seen him at all since her funeral. He's a friend of the family, and I hear he still visits my parents sometimes. Even after he got a new girlfriend, he still comes. After all this time. And they say he wants to see me. But I'll never see him again as long as I live. I don't ever want to remember what I felt then. And that goes for whoever else I might feel that way about."

"So when you see that someone like Takano has feelings for you . . ."

"I get frightened and I run away. I want to scream at him to stop it. I'm not the kind of person who can be loved. I try to live my life guarding against the possibility of anyone falling in love with me. But Takano is always so kind and pure. I'm afraid I let myself take advantage of that a little. And because of that, I ended up hurting his feelings. I'm the worst. I need to apologize to him when I see him."

"I don't know, Tomo. Doesn't it make you sad to live like that?"

"When I'm sad, I read. I can go on reading for hours. Reading quiets the turmoil I feel inside and brings me peace. Because when I'm immersed in the world of a book, no one can get hurt," Tomo said and smiled. But her smile made her look sadder than I'd ever seen her before. Or maybe after I'd made up my mind early on that she was this cheerful, good-natured girl, I never once thought to look at what lay beneath the surface.

But now that I knew, was there something I could say that could thaw her frozen heart?

In reality, after she smiled for me and said, "Thank you for listening. I feel a little better," I couldn't say anything in response. It was too painful to realize that this was the reason she read so much. All I could do was remember the pain that seemed to squeeze itself deep inside my chest.

It was a drizzly evening, two days after I went to Tomo's place. I was on my way home after dropping by the Morisaki Bookshop. Wada and I didn't have any plans to meet, so I stopped at my second-favorite coffee shop, Kissaku. What Tomo had told me was still swirling around inside me, and I was in a dark mood. I didn't feel like going straight home.

After idling away almost an hour there, I decided it was time to go, so I opened my umbrella and started walking on the avenue heading to Jimbocho Station when the figure of a man walking a little ahead of me caught my eye. Seeing him from behind in that familiar jacket . . . it was Wada, without a doubt. He must be on his way home after work.

I jogged after him, and I was about to call his name, when Wada stopped right in front of a drugstore at the traffic light. And then a young woman came rushing over and stood in front of him. It looked as if they'd planned to meet each other there.

I only caught a glimpse of her face in profile underneath her red umbrella, but I knew right away who it was. Without a doubt, it was the woman Wada went out with before me. The way she was dressed, the way she looked—she hadn't changed at all from the last time I saw her at the Morisaki Bookshop.

The two of them seemed to be discussing something. Wada looked at her and nodded. I promptly hid behind the sign of a restaurant. I had no idea why I felt the need to hide, but that's what I found myself doing. And while I was hiding, the two of them walked away, side by side.

What was I doing? I asked myself that question as I walked behind them, leaving a little distance between us. Am I just going to follow them? I thought it over. It was true though. If I wasn't tailing them, then what could I call what I was doing? In the light rain, Yasukuni Street was so full of men and women holding umbrellas on their way home from work that there was no reason to believe Wada and his ex would notice me. The two of them kept walking along the road, paused for a moment, and then walked into a Doutor coffee shop like it was a perfectly appropriate thing to do.

I walked back and forth in front of the entrance for a while, thinking they might come out soon. As I wandered aimlessly in front of the coffee shop, salarymen passed by on their way home from work, casting sidelong glances at me like I was in their way.

I might have stayed for ten minutes. In my head, I felt calm, but I was also terribly confused. Looking around, I saw the rain had mostly stopped. The people walking down the street had closed their umbrellas.

I could hear myself muttering as I put away my umbrella. Then I trudged wearily back to the station.

10

What happened that evening hit me harder than expected. I felt restless during the day, and at night I couldn't sleep. I didn't feel much like reading.

It got so bad that at work I made a ridiculous mistake, and they discovered a major problem with the data I sent to a client. That caused me to get yelled at mercilessly by Wada #2. But it was all 100 percent my fault.

I was utterly useless. I couldn't concentrate on anything.

At night in my apartment, when I was all alone on my futon, I couldn't stop going over these foolish things in my head.

What did it mean to be in a relationship? I wondered as I stared vacantly at the ceiling. We went to the movies, we went out to eat, we slept at each other's places. But if I never got inside his heart, would we ever really be together? What exactly did I mean to Wada? For example, did I have the right to interrogate him about what happened that night? Even thinking of it as a right made me feel like there was something wrong with me.

Because of all this, I was afraid even to talk to Wada. I used to look forward to his calls, but now I wanted to run and hide when I saw his name show up on my phone.

Wada's voice still sounded exactly the same on the phone after that night. Calm and kind as always. Before, whenever I heard his voice, I felt at ease. Like I was looking out over the calm surface of a lake. But now, his voice felt awfully far away.

"What's wrong?" Wada asked me, sounding worried. But I was never good at expressing myself. "Are you not feeling well?" I could hear in his voice that he was confused.

"No. It's nothing. Well, good night."

Right before I hung up, I told him I had to cancel our date next week because I was going to be working late.

Soon, I'd reached my limit for being stuck in my head and depressed. I found myself heading toward the little restaurant where Momoko worked.

"Oh dear, you mean Wada would do something so shameless?"

I'd told her that all this had happened to a friend of mine, but Momoko saw through me easily. There was no way I was going to pull one over on her. While she watched over me in her white apron, I drank sake, and then the words came easily, as if the tangled thread inside me had come loose at last. I came clean about the whole story, including how I still couldn't get over it.

"Good grief, this place is turning into a relationship counseling service."

"I'm sorry."

"Well, as long as it's for my adorable niece," Momoko said with a grin, though I had my doubts whether she truly meant it. "You're afraid to confirm this with Wada?" she asked.

I nodded silently.

"But Wada's not that kind of person, is he?"

"It's because I believe he isn't that kind of person that it's so scary. Because the thought that he could cheat on me is really terrifying."

"Hey, Takako." Momoko came around from behind the counter and sat down next to me. "Listen, I'm no great scholar. I'm not very well-read. It's all I can do to read one book in the time Satoru reads ten. But I think I'm a pretty good judge of people. As far as I can tell, Wada would never deliberately hurt you. You can see that in his eyes. But I think maybe the bigger problem here is the wall you've built around yourself."

"The wall?" I repeated.

Sitting beside me, Momoko stared at me, trying to look me right in the eye.

"You know what I mean, don't you?"

"I think I might."

After what happened with my previous boyfriend, I had unconsciously been avoiding trusting anyone completely. And I was scared, scared because I'd been careless in trusting someone before, scared of being hurt again, of cursing myself for my own foolishness and wanting to throw it all away again.

That's why I was always overreacting to everything Wada said or did, and not just on this occasion.

"*If you won't* open your heart, it's selfish to expect the other person alone to open theirs to you, don't you think?" Momoko said. "Unless you take that first step, I don't think anything's going to get better. Wada's a human being, after all. He might get tired of living with your chronic indecisiveness, and if that happens, you'll be the one to regret it."

What Momoko said cut me to the quick. I'd asked so much of Wada, but I hadn't offered anything in return. And like she said, I had gone to great pains to read into every little thing Wada did or said, searching for what the look in his eyes could have told me.

As I mulled this over, I heard a high-pitched shriek coming from the kitchen. Mr. Nakasono, the owner, was yelling, "Momoko, help me!"

"Yes, right away," Momoko shouted back, and got up from her chair.

"Well, I've got to run, but do me a favor and try not to worry your aunt Momoko too much. Hurry up and put my mind at ease." She pinched my cheek, and without giving me a moment to respond, she ran at full speed to the kitchen, where Mr. Nakasono was still yelling, "Help! Help!"

It was Thursday night, a few days later, that we held Tomo's birthday party. We called it a party, but it was a cozy night with just the three of us. At Tomo's request, we'd decided to have dinner on the second floor of the Morisaki Bookshop, and had brought the long table normally used as a counter upstairs to set up our hot pot.

We tried to invite my uncle and Momoko, but they declined, claiming the party "was no place for old folks like them." Takano refused to come at first, saying that Tomo probably wouldn't want him there, but I persuaded him that it wasn't true, and half forced him to join us. He showed up with a nervous look on his face, dressed lightly, of course, in only an orange hooded sweatshirt. I couldn't help thinking that he ought to have dressed a little more stylishly for a night with the girl he loved.

Although Tomo knew that Takano was coming, the two of them only said hello at the door to the bookshop and seemed awkwardly nervous after that. I couldn't say things were great with Wada, but things were looking really bad here, so I forced myself to be cheerful. My cheerfulness was purely superficial though, and it only seemed to end up dampening the mood further.

In this gloomy atmosphere, we picked at the hot pot, barely saying a word. Takano and I drank beer while Tomo, who didn't drink alcohol, had orange juice. Tomo ate only vegetables; Takano ate only tofu.

But we've done all this for Tomo's birthday, I thought to myself. As I watched the two of them sitting there silently with only their chopsticks moving, I got more and more irritated. And naturally, the one to bear the brunt of my irritation was Takano.

"Takano, can you quit eating only the tofu? Eat some vegetables and chicken."

Takano had just taken two big, round pieces of tofu and was eating them by himself.

"What? Oh, I'm sorry. I just thought there was too much tofu left. I assumed you two didn't really like it." Takano was flustered, but I kept pushing him.

"Don't make that decision on your own. I'm trying to eat a nice balanced meal. Tomo, you want some tofu too, don't you?"

Tomo was startled as she was suddenly drawn into the conversation. She looked up at us. "No, I'm fine," she said. "Takano, you can eat it."

"You can't be too polite, Tomo. It's your birthday," I said.

Takano nodded frantically in agreement. "That's right. I promise not to touch another piece of tofu. Please eat as much as you like."

He was about to put the tofu slices back, so I rushed to stop him.

After that, we left our leading lady alone and went back and forth bickering over tofu. Tomo watched us, looking like she had no idea what to do. In the end, just after I complained that Takano was a guy who couldn't even dress for the season, Tomo couldn't take it anymore and intervened.

"Um, the tofu is really not a problem. What's more important is I need to apologize to Takano," she said, turning to face him. "I was awful to you. It's entirely my fault. I'm sorry," she said, bowing deeply.

Takano panicked, as one might have expected, and at the moment he tried to stand up he banged his kneecap on the corner of the table.

"No, please, I'm the one who needs to apologize," he said, in agony from his throbbing knee. Tomo apologized again. As I cleaned up the mess Takano had made of the table, I said to both of them, "Let's leave it at that, shall we?"

Takano had tears in his eyes, from his feelings for Tomo or from the pain in his knee, and he seemed to want to say something else, but he reluctantly sat down and stopped talking.

In any case, after that the heaviness in the air seemed to dissipate. I seized the chance to give Tomo her birthday presents. Mine was a brooch in the shape of a lily that I thought she might like; Takano's was a stained-glass lamp. The lamp was intricately crafted in the shape of a lighthouse. It was kind of a wonderful item, the kind of thing a guy who wore seasonally appropriate clothes might choose. Tomo smiled at last, and said both presents were wonderful.

"Actually, Takano originally wanted to give you a different present," I said, ignoring Takano's attempts to stop me. There was no need to keep it a secret now. "But we couldn't find the book, Tomo. *The Golden Dream*. You've been looking for it all this time, right?"

Tomo's mouth hung open. She looked flabbergasted. She turned to me and asked wildly, "What? You were looking for that book?"

"Well, yeah, but . . ."

"I apologize. I'd always remembered what you said about it back at the Saveur. I guess I went too far," Takano said. "I'm sorry."

Tomo looked flabbergasted again as she listened to Takano. "No, it's not that, Takano. That book doesn't actually exist."

Now it was our turn to be shocked.

"What? Really? But . . ."

"I'm sorry. I described it in a way that invited this misunderstanding."

"But when Takano looked it up online, he found a post from other people who were searching for it too." Takano nodded along with me.

"That must've been other people who believed it existed too. In part, it's become almost a rumor. You could think of it as a phantom book," Tomo said apologetically.

In that case there was no way we could have found it even searching in the greatest neighborhood for books in the world. It was no wonder my uncle didn't know it either. Leave it to Takano to jump to conclusions like that. I gave Takano a look full of loathing as he sat there astonished. Then again, I never had the slightest suspicion that the book might not exist so I couldn't lay the blame entirely on Takano.

In any case, Tomo gave us a detailed account of the book that did not exist.

In the early years of the Showa era, an unknown writer named Mitsuko Fuyuno published a book called *A Moment of Twilight*. It's the story of an isolated and blind old man, who is facing death, and the middle-aged woman he hires to read to him. Perhaps the story was too romantic, because neither the literary world nor the general public paid any attention at the time of its publication. *The Golden Dream* is the novel the woman reads to the old man when he's on his deathbed. That text is the key to the whole book. At the time, there were a number of people who became obsessed with finding it, and among them it was a bit of a craze. But after several years, they established that the book was actually the author's creation.

"In *A Moment of Twilight*, *The Golden Dream* is described as a breathtaking masterpiece. After the book is read to him, the novel ends with the old man, who up till then had never known love, realizing that the woman at his side, who had served as his eyes for many years, is the person he's in love with.

"It was my sister who first told me about the novel *The Golden Dream*. She said it was a wonderful book, and I absolutely had to read it. This was about half a year before the accident. I always believed everything my sister told me. So I was fixated on finding that book. But then I discovered that no such book actually existed . . ."

Tomo turned to me and laughed like it was all a joke.

"It seems likely that my sister knew from the start that the book didn't exist. I mean she said she'd borrowed the book from her boyfriend and read it.

"Why would my sister lie to me? My sister wasn't the kind of person to lie about insignificant things. So then why? Was it only to make fun of me? Or maybe she had noticed my forbidden love I felt for her boyfriend, and she wanted to pay me back? Either way, now that my sister's dead, there's no way I'll ever know.

"And even though there is no book, I still find myself looking for it whenever I go into a used bookshop. Whenever someone asks me if there's a book I want, it's always the first thing I mention. Some part of me hopes that if I ever find that book, something inside me will change, like the old blind man in the book. I know it's an extremely infantile thing to believe, but still . . ."

"I had absolutely no idea you were looking for that book. I'm really sorry." At the end, Tomo apologized to us again.

"There's no need to apologize. After all, we took it upon ourselves to look for it."

To think that we spent two weeks searching for the book without the slightest idea of the real story behind it. It all seemed perfectly meaningless now. Tomo wasn't just looking for that book. Deep down, she was searching for an answer she'd never find. And it was all connected to events around her sister's death. Or rather, she was trying to connect it to them.

When Tomo talked about her sister she always gave that lonesome smile. She seemed so sad.

"Happy birthday!" Takano suddenly stood up and yelled. "Your smile always gave me courage. I never quit my job and tried to do my best at the coffee shop because I wanted to see your smile." What was this guy talking about all of a sudden? I tugged hard on his sleeve still in shock, but he was so excited, I couldn't stop him.

"I mean, what I'm trying to say is that, even if you didn't realize it, you helped someone, and that person is here right now with you. Someone who's sincerely happy to be with you on the day that you were born is standing right here with you now. I want you to remember that if you can. That's all I wanted to say." After saying all that without pausing to breathe, he ended by uttering another feeble "Happy birthday." Then his face turned bright red like he was angry, and he sat down with a thud. All at once the room fell silent. He wanted to cheer up Tomo so badly it hurt, but I think, no matter how you look at it, this might have been too much at once.

In front of us, the hot pot had reached a rolling boil, so I turned off the flame on the burner. Tomo hadn't opened her mouth. She was still looking down, staring into her lap.

Then she slowly got to her feet. She opened the sliding door to the room buried under the book collection, went in, and suddenly slid the door shut from the inside.

"Did I say something wrong?"

There was no sound coming from the room next door. We waited for a moment, but she didn't seem to be coming out. I was worried, so I knocked on the door and peeked inside. I had no idea why, but there in the dim light, Tomo was sitting upright, reading with intense concentration. Even though I had opened the door, she made no attempt to look my way.

"Um, Tomo?" I said with her back toward me.

"Yes?"

"What are you doing?"

"What do you mean? I'm reading," she replied, sounding perfectly composed.

"Yeah, but why now?"

"I felt a sudden urge to read," she said without looking up from the book. Was this her way of avoiding reality? The reality that Takano's speech could be seen as a declaration of love?

As Takano drew near to her from behind, Tomo brought her face closer to her book, as if she were trying to immerse herself in reading even more. Takano and I turned toward each other, but we had absolutely no idea what to do.

Then before I knew it, Takano abruptly sat down beside Tomo, grabbed a nearby paperback, and began to read in silence.

For an instant, Tomo looked up and saw Takano, then she returned to her book without saying a word.

"What? . . . You're scaring me . . ." I muttered aloud without meaning to. Neither of them showed the slightest reaction. I started to worry a little about what I'd do if I was stuck waiting for them like this until morning.

Takano abruptly opened his mouth to speak. "Um . . . Tomoko, I'm not good at explaining myself. I might not know how to say this, but I can stay with you like this without talking. You call when you need me. I'll come right away."

Tomo didn't look up from her book, but there was a slight stirring in the shadows. It even seemed like she nodded slightly. When Takano saw this, he smiled a little and then went back to reading silently.

Surprising as it may seem, perhaps it was Takano who understood Tomo, or maybe even human beings in general, far better than I did. While I was worrying about how I could bring them together, he was thinking about how to make her feel better. Rather than trying to force open the door that she had wanted closed behind her, it made more sense to start by getting her to open it from her side. Maybe he's right, I thought. As I watched the two of them sitting silently side by side, it seemed that someday soon Tomo might open the door herself.

I picked up a nearby book and leaned against the wall. As I flipped through the pages, I reached a decision. I would call Wada. I would tell him that I wanted to see him soon. I had to be the one to tear down the wall I'd built.

As it grew late on the night of Tomo's birthday party, the only sound was the turning of pages.

11

Because of a typhoon that swept across Western Japan, we had days of strong rain and wind. The trees on the streets lost most of their leaves. They looked a little embarrassed with their bare branches sticking up into the sky.

Wada was very busy at work for a while, and it wasn't until four days after Tomo's birthday party that we were able to see each other. Normally, it would have been his day off, but Wada had to rush to work and stayed into the afternoon. It was close to evening by the time we met.

Apparently Wada thought that I'd been acting strangely recently. As soon as we were together, he asked me apprehensively if something was wrong. I decided I would ask first about what happened that night.

After I'd finished telling him what I saw, Wada murmured, "So, is that the reason you've seemed so down?" He seemed to understand at last. "It's no wonder," he said. He let out a long sigh, as if he realized he'd made a terrible mistake. Then he sat there with his eyes shut, not moving at all.

The Saveur was packed again that day. Sitting next to us, a man in a suit sipped his coffee as he leisurely spread out his newspaper on the table. Across from us, a young couple huddled together talking. The rain had cleared up early that morning, and the sun was peeking through the clouds at last. Through the window, the soft dusk light quietly streamed into the dimly lit interior.

Wada hadn't touched his coffee. He sat there with a grim expression on his face. His shoulder, closer to the window, glowed gold in the sunlight. He hadn't moved in so long that I began to worry. "Are you okay?" I asked.

Wada opened his eyes, and sounding even more serious than usual, he said, "I'm okay . . . I was wrong not to tell you about it. It was thoughtless. I don't know. I just imagined it from your point of view, and I thought it would make you feel bad. But it looks like, by not telling you, I ended up worrying you instead. I'm really sorry." Wada said all this incredibly fast. He tried to recount the sequence of events that led to him seeing her . . . That evening when he was at work, she'd contacted him out of the blue, saying she wanted to return a book of his. It was the first time he'd heard from her in a year. He said she could keep it, but she said she was already nearby, and she insisted on returning it. When he met up with her, she urged him to come back to her . . .

But before Wada could say more, I interrupted him. "That's enough."

"Enough?" he said, his eyes wide with surprise.

"I mean it's okay. I see clearly that it was nothing," I said, smiling. The smile came naturally; there was no need to force it. To tell the truth, I'd been pretty anxious about seeing Wada again. But with him right in front of me, I felt so much better somehow, and it really seemed things were okay.

"What? But . . ." Wada furrowed his brow. The look on his face showed he didn't understand how I'd been convinced so quickly. He always made that face whenever he was baffled by something. The man sitting next to us looked up from his newspaper, reacting perhaps to the sound of Wada's voice, and gave us a glance. But he quickly lost interest and went back to his own little world.

"It wasn't because I wanted you to tell me about that that I asked to see you today. The truth is, I just wanted to see you."

"But you were worrying about it."

I shook my head. "It really doesn't matter. It was a shock, for sure, but the biggest shock for me was that it made me realize I didn't trust you. I wasn't sure how to face you today . . . So, you see, I was the problem, not you."

"The problem?" Wada frowned again. It was starting to seem like he'd been making that face all day.

"That's right. Because I was a coward. I've been holding back from opening my heart to you. Without realizing it, I was afraid of getting hurt. I finally understood when Momoko pointed it out to me. That's why I've decided to put an end to all that."

Once I put it into words, it felt like all the pointless anxiety that had been building up in my body was suddenly released. I felt at ease. It was okay. Really. I could see that when I took a good look at Wada. I hadn't tried that before. Not once in the whole time we'd been going out.

Wada stared at me for a long time, blinking again and again, before he finally mumbled, "Is that right?" He sounded deeply moved.

"Hmmm?" I asked.

"I was just thinking that you spent this week thinking all this for me," he said, and finally brought the coffee to his lips.

"Hmmm," I said, leaning my head to one side as I thought it over. "Maybe it was for you, or maybe it was really for me. If I hadn't done that, I think at some point I would've started to hate myself. If that happened, I wouldn't be able to be with you. And I couldn't have that."

Wada listened to me, scratching his head. He gave an embarrassed laugh. "I feel like I've been on a roller coaster today."

"I'm sorry. I think it all must sound weird," I said, and finished the last of my coffee, signaling that we'd reached the end of that part of the conversation.

Before we left the coffee shop, Wada, conscientious to a fault, added one last thing, fidgeting a little as he spoke: "It's really my fault. Anyway, there's nothing going on with her. I won't see her again. Believe me." I couldn't help letting out a little laugh.

After that, Wada and I took a long stroll through the neighborhood at twilight. We were headed to his place. We both had to be at work in the morning, but tonight we wanted to be together.

Wada was walking along as he always did, with his back straight and his head held high, when he suddenly said, "Can I confess something? I'm really jealous of you, Takako."

"Me? Why?" I asked. What he'd said was so unexpected it astonished me.

"You have so many people you can rely on, so many people you can trust."

"You mean people like my uncle Satoru?"

"Yes," he nodded with a smile. "It's obvious. You mean so much to everyone."

"You think so?" It's not that I hadn't felt it before, though I'd felt there were a lot of people who liked to make fun of me. Especially Momoko and Sabu.

"It's because you draw all of these people to you. You have that magnetism. And because you value them too."

"I'm not so sure about magnetism," I said, embarrassed. "But it's true that after I came up to Tokyo, there weren't many people in my life whom I'd known for very long. It was the same when I was at home too. I didn't really have anyone I could speak to freely the way

I can with my uncle and Momoko or people like Tomo. I'm kind of amazed by it myself."

When I first went to my uncle's bookshop, I never dreamed I'd meet all these people. That includes Wada too. If not for my pathetic broken heart, I never would've come to the Morisaki Bookshop, and I would still be estranged from my uncle, and I probably would never have met Wada. Thinking about it made me feel strange. It was all interconnected, and now we were walking side by side through the streets of Jimbocho at twilight.

But the idea that Wada felt jealous of me was still hard to imagine. And Wada was someone who could endear himself to a multitude of people no matter where we went. He was the kind of person who could get along well with everyone.

Wada strongly disagreed when I told him what I thought. "That's not true at all. From the time I was little, people always told me I was so serious. It's true that I might be able to get along well with people anywhere I go, but on the other hand, I'm constantly positioning myself as an outsider, and I can't do more than interact with people. My mind is always calm. I don't really have many memories of joy, even as a child. I don't know why that is. I think it might be the effect of growing up in an emotionally distant home. I distanced myself from my parents at times, but I don't think that was the only reason for it. I was probably just born like that. It's just the kind of person I am." Wada went on talking, his eyes fixed on the palm of his right hand, like he was trying to see what he was made of. "Everyone gets tired of being with a person like that, even if there's a novelty to it at first. It doesn't matter who it is. That's why everyone ends up going away. The first time you saw my place, it was in a terrible condition, wasn't it? I don't know. I think it shows what kind of person I am. For all the ways I've learned to keep up appearances, on the inside I'm a mess. And there's nothing I can do about it.

"But when I look at you and the Morisakis, deep down I know I want to be a part of that world. It's what I long for. The idea I told you about—to write a novel set at the bookshop—I think that was my own modest way of trying to be a part of it." As Wada said those words, he looked at me. He seemed a little bit embarrassed. I found myself looking back at him, staring at his face. Until this moment, I hadn't the slightest idea that he felt this way. I felt like I finally understood why he'd looked so anxious when he confessed that he was writing a novel.

"I want all of you to accept me. I want to share the joy and sadness with all of you. This is really the first time in my life I've felt that way."

I gently squeezed Wada's warm hand in mine.

"Of course, we will. I mean, you're a wonderful person."

"You think so?" Wada muttered without any conviction.

I turned to look at him and said definitively, "You are. I promise."

Wada looked at me, a bit surprised, and smiled fondly. "Thank you," he said. But I felt like I was the one who ought to thank him. I was happy that Wada had told me how he felt. I was happy he cared about me and the people who are important to me. I kind of felt like I was being rewarded. For finding the courage to confide in him what I was feeling.

Sharing your thoughts with someone seems so simple, but at times it can be surprisingly difficult. Even more so when it's someone you care so much for. That's what I thought about as I walked next to him. But if you can find the courage to do it, it'll bring you closer together.

We turned the corner, and Wada's apartment building came into view. We walked straight for it, hand in hand.

In the space of a few days, it felt like winter had arrived, and my favorite season was over. But that wasn't so bad.

Because from here on, whether it was winter or spring or whatever season might come, I believed these gentle days would continue. And all the people I love would spend them laughing together.

As we walked down the street at twilight, this was what I told myself, though I had no grounds to believe it.

12

I have something to tell you.

It was past the middle of December when Uncle Satoru suddenly made this announcement. I had come into the Morisaki Bookshop in the morning on my day off. With one thing or another, I hadn't been there in two weeks. The hours before closing went by peacefully, but just as I was getting ready to leave, my uncle called me over. "Do you have a minute?" my uncle said, looking ill at ease.

"Sure, that's fine, but . . ." Recently, my uncle had become a little bit more taciturn, compared to earlier. I was concerned without really knowing why. To be honest, with everything going on with Wada and Tomo and the normal everyday busyness, I hadn't been paying much attention to it. Still, my uncle had definitely seemed odd recently. More than anything, just for him to say that he had something to tell me was weird. If he wanted to tell me something, he was the kind of person who would just come out and say it.

We decided that first the two of us would work together and quickly close the shop, and then we'd go out.

The moment we were outside, we could feel the cold night air on our cheeks. A pure, unadulterated winter night. The kind of night where everything around seems quieter, and the air makes you shiver all over. Stars were shining in the black sky.

"Shall we walk a little?" I suggested. I thought it might make us feel better to breathe the air outside and move around a little.

"But aren't you cold?"

"That's why I want to walk a bit."

"Well, then let's do it together."

We left Sakura Street, turned after coming out onto the avenue, and then followed the road. For someone with short legs, my uncle walks pretty quickly, and there was no way he was going to attempt to match his pace to that of a less fleet-footed person. As a result, when we walked together, the gap between us would widen step by step. But I knew that after we'd gone a certain distance, he would always stop and wait for me, so I never needed to rush. I went at my own relaxed pace, following behind my uncle, with his back to me. It was just like the old days. Whenever we went for a walk when I was a child, I would end up following him with my eyes as his skinny little back went on ahead of me.

When we came to the moat of the Imperial Palace, we decided to take a rest before heading back.

In the moat, the streetlights shone dimly on the surface of the water, where a black, silhouetted bird swam by gracefully. Back behind the hedges, the Imperial Palace looked dark and deserted. My uncle bought us two bottles of Hot Lemon and passed one of them to me. "This is so you won't catch a cold," he said.

That was another thing that hadn't changed since the old days: he still liked Hot Lemon.

"Ooh boy," my uncle said wearily as he sat down on one of the benches lined up along the moat.

I smirked and said, "Is your butt okay?"

"Ah, this is nothing." He gave me a thumbs-up.

From there, we had a good view of the night sky. We could see the slender crescent moon, and a little past that, the twinkling stars of Orion. There were still many lights on in the newspaper building across from the Imperial Palace. Along the avenue parallel to the moat, runners ran, gasping for breath. My uncle and I sipped our Hot Lemons, now and then letting our gaze follow a passing runner.

"Thanks, by the way, for the trip. All in all, I'm glad we went. Momoko was happy. When I think about it, maybe it hadn't been ten years since we'd gone on a trip like that."

The trip was over a month ago, but my uncle was just telling me this now.

"You're welcome. Thank you for always looking out for me."

"Nah, I don't do all that much."

I looked up at the night sky and said, "You've been looking after me since I was a kid." I got a little embarrassed thinking about how well he knew me as a child.

"Is that right? I guess we've known each other for more than twenty years altogether." My uncle and I were both staring up at the sky now, squinting as we looked back with nostalgia. "Time goes by quickly, doesn't it?"

"Well, we didn't see each other for a long time. To tell you the truth, once I got to puberty, I really couldn't stand you. I couldn't figure out what you were thinking. You were old enough to know better, but you were always just dithering around."

"That's harsh. I'm in shock." My uncle gave the same flat laugh he always did, his breath forming round white cottony shapes in the air.

"Sorry. But when I was a kid, I adored you. When I think back to those times, I have only happy memories. I can see now just how kind you were to me."

He laughed. "But then you hated me and I didn't realize it. And I guess that's why you didn't come see me for quite a long time."

"I didn't hate you. I just had trouble dealing with you. But I don't feel that way at all now."

"That's a good thing, I guess, but . . ."

As we talked, for some reason I remembered that uncomfortable feeling again. Beside me, my uncle was laughing the way he always laughed, and talking the way he always talked. His kind voice was the same as always. But something was definitely different. He was perplexed about something. Spending a quiet evening together like this, I could feel it distinctly, and it left me deeply worried. And then, deep inside my chest, the feeling grew a little stronger.

"Um, Uncle, what was it you wanted to tell me?" I hesitated to ask the question, but my uncle didn't seem like he was going to get to the point on his own.

"Ah, yes."

"I'm guessing maybe it's not very good news?"

I realized that I was tightly squeezing the plastic bottle in my hand. Although my body was cold, my hands were sweating. My uncle glanced at me from the corner of his eye, and then nodded slightly.

"Well, I guess not."

"So, what is it?"

My uncle nodded again. "Actually," he said with a serious look on his face. "My hemorrhoids are really hurting me something fierce again. No, really, it's gotten to be a serious problem."

I was a fool to be so worried. Without saying a word, I gave him a big shove with both hands. As he was about to fall from the bench, he gave a weird shriek. "Ta . . . Takako, what are you doing? I'm begging you, please don't give my butt any more excitement."

"Jerk."

I let out a big sigh, like I was releasing all the stress that had been building inside me. I felt both incredibly angry and incredibly relieved. Is that right? All this is about your hemorrhoids? I thought to myself. They hurt. I'm sure it's terrible, but if that's all it is, we're lucky. Really lucky.

"Tomorrow," I said, "you've absolutely got to go to the hospital."

"Okay, I'll do it."

"Absolutely."

I sprang to my feet and said, "Well, should we get going?" If we didn't get home soon, we really were going to catch a cold. But my uncle made no attempt to get up from the bench. Did his hemorrhoids hurt that badly? I guess that's how it goes. I reached out my right hand to try to pull him up.

However, my uncle just sat there staring at my hand; he made no attempt to take hold of it. When I got impatient and called out, "Hey," he muttered, "It's about Momoko."

"Huh?" I replied, taken aback.

"Actually, she told me when we were on that trip." He pursed his lips then, as if to pause for a moment. Then he slowly opened his mouth again and went on. "She said the cancer came back before all that. She'd found out much earlier from her doctor. But she couldn't say anything about it for a long time. And, she, um, said it's pretty advanced."

My uncle's breath turned white, floated up into the sky, and then vanished.

"I'm still the only person who knows, but sooner or later everyone's going to find out. Before that happens, I thought I'd just tell you . . ."

I was struck then by the strange sensation that the ground had suddenly been yanked out from under my feet. I was having trouble standing. My hands and feet suddenly felt cold. The hand I was still holding out to my uncle, now, without my willing it, went limp and drooped down.

"That isn't true, is it? It can't be. I mean, she looks so healthy . . ."

I wanted it to not be true. I was pleading with him. But it was true. The misery in his eyes said it all.

13

A flock of migrating birds flew across the featureless winter sky. They formed a single column, propelling themselves with big flaps of their black wings. When it seemed they'd risen high in the sky, they circled and receded into the distance, carried by the wind until finally they were only tiny black specks that vanished into the clouds.

Where were they going?

I contemplated the question as I gazed at the birds from the hospital window.

The winds were strong today. They'd built a relatively large courtyard in the hospital, where the patients could take walks. On warm days, you'd often see people there, but no one was out today. The fierce wind blew through the line of pine trees, bending their branches till they creaked wildly. Cold outside air poured in through the window I'd left slightly ajar.

"See something interesting?"

When I looked, I saw Momoko, sitting up in bed, peacefully knitting as she watched me standing at the window. I closed the window gently.

"No, I was just noticing how windy it is today. Is it okay that I shut the window?"

"It's fine. Thanks."

Momoko's knitting needles moved lightly back and forth in a nice rhythm. Lately, she seemed to be lost in her knitting, her gaze focused always on her hands.

"What are you knitting?"

"Gloves."

"Even though it's the end of February?"

"It's okay. I'm only doing it for my own enjoyment. It's perfect for killing time."

"Hmmm . . ." I sat down on the folding chair beside her, and the two of us watched her hands as she knit.

"Takako? Could I give you these? I don't need gloves."

"Sure. I could use them. But how long will they take to finish?"

"I might be done in March? But you could wear them again next year too, right?"

Next year.

I repeated the word to myself. It was impossible to imagine that Momoko might not be with us next year. Or rather, I didn't want to imagine it. Trying to negate that unpleasant thought, I said cheerfully, "Yes, please."

"Got it."

She lifted her head for a moment and gave me a smile. A perfectly innocent smile, overflowing with affection. She was staying in a four-person room at a general hospital in the city. She'd had surgery before in the same hospital. The room she stayed in then was different, but apparently it was on the same floor. At that time, she was still separated from my uncle, so she would've had no one at her side. It must've been so lonely.

The room itself smelled of medications and that antiseptic particular to hospitals, and also slightly of sweat. Behind the cream-colored curtain, the walls were bright white. A little bit cold and indifferent. "That's what hospitals are like," Momoko said. She had an exasperated look on her face, as if to say, "That's just how things are."

"Well, you should go home. I can't bear you sitting there forever."

Momoko gestured with her chin toward the door. Her hands never stopped moving. When I came to visit her at the hospital, she always sent me home within the hour like this. I couldn't tell if she was doing it for my sake or if I was really annoying her.

"You don't need to look after me like that. As you can see, I'm fine," she always said at the end of my visits, giving a little snort. I'd end up leaving the hospital like I'd been shooed away.

But Momoko's complexion was good, and her skin was firm—she looked like the picture of health. She ate up all the food they brought her, and even in bed her posture was as good as always. It's strange to say this, but there was so little change in her appearance it almost seemed anticlimactic.

On the night I went for that long walk with my uncle, he kept grumbling all the way back, "She's such a troublemaker," sighing a little each time. We walked along the road to the station, shoulder to shoulder, moving slowly as if it were against the law to walk any faster. I have absolutely no memory of the route we followed from the Imperial Palace. But afterward, I could still hear the sound of him quietly sighing as if he couldn't keep his emotions from overflowing from inside him.

Then I came to know a few things I'd never imagined could be true.

Momoko's cancer was already fairly advanced; they had detected that it was already spreading through her lymph nodes, which meant surgery would be difficult. That's what the doctors had informed her. Momoko had accepted this and didn't want to undergo another surgery. At first, my uncle had protested vehemently, but after repeatedly meeting with the attending physician, he started to think that might be for the best. For him, the most important thing was to respect Momoko's wishes.

Walking beside him, I could only respond listlessly with a "Yes" or "Is that right?" Caught off guard by this sudden news, I couldn't gather my thoughts. I didn't know what to think. As I listened to my uncle talk, the only thing I understood was that the situation was far more serious than I'd thought.

The sound of my uncle sighing blurred together with the sound of passing cars. For a while, I just stared at the asphalt without saying a word.

"You said she told you on the trip, right?" I asked, suddenly preoccupied by this possibility.

"Yeah, she dropped it on me with no warning. I was shocked. I mean you know how she jokes around a lot, but she would never joke about something like that. I realized pretty soon that she was serious."

"So, you've known for a long time." All I'd wanted was for that trip to be a chance for the two of them to rest. To think that this was what they were talking about. Looking back, I realized that it was after that trip that my uncle became noticeably quiet. He held that secret in his heart for a long time without saying a word. I could sense how difficult it was for him to tell me. To say it aloud would mean fully accepting the truth. That had to be scary.

"It must've been hard for you to be the only one who knew," I said.

"Nah, not really." He laughed dryly.

"Like I told you, it's not something that's going to happen right away. In a little while, she'll probably have to go to the hospital. And then they'll have to see how things go from there.

"Oh, I see . . ." So when he said they weren't going to operate, it wasn't that she was going to make a full recovery—it meant she didn't have much time left.

That came as the biggest shock for me. The thought that the disease lurking inside her would soon grab hold of her and carry her away from us to the other side. That before long, Momoko would be gone from this world. It was impossible to believe such a thing. I'd already let myself imagine the kind of sweet old lady she would be one day. And I imagined that she would run the Morisaki Bookshop forever together with my uncle, who would've aged like her and turned into an old man.

I realized I was sighing softly now just like my uncle. As if on cue, my uncle muttered, "I give up. Just when I thought she'd come home after five years, it turns out she's sick. And even worse, we're nearly at the terminal stage. She's acting like nothing's happening, so it hasn't sunk in yet at all. It would help if she could let herself act a little more like a patient."

My uncle shook his head miserably and let out another little sigh.

"Yeah," I said.

"I can't win with her."

He said it again and again until we made it to the station.

But for a long time after that, the days went by as if nothing had happened, just as my uncle had said. At the bookshop, Momoko looked after the customers, just as she always did, and a few days each week, she went over to help at the little restaurant nearby. Sabu and the other regulars were always stopping by the bookshop, looking for Momoko's polite smile. On the surface, not a thing had changed.

Even when I went to see her at the bookshop after I knew about her illness, her response was matter-of-fact.

"Well, that's how it goes," she said, sounding unconcerned.

"But, um . . ."

I wanted to say something, but before I could open my mouth, she said, "There's just nothing we can do about it. I'm prepared. And I'm halfway ready for it. So please don't look at me with that grim expression on your face. You'll end up getting me down too," she said, smiling, and slapped me on the back. It felt like she was the one cheering me up.

Since she herself was acting that way, it didn't seem right for me to be depressed.

The day was coming, but until it arrived, I felt strongly that I wanted to spend as much time as possible being Momoko's niece, and her friend, however far apart we were in age. And I needed to be of help to my aunt and uncle in whatever way I could.

And then, a little while later, they decided it was time for Momoko to be hospitalized. It happened after the start of the new year.

At first, it was supposed to be temporary, but they said it could become long-term depending on her condition. She explained the situation to Mr. Nakasono, and she took the rest of January off from working at the restaurant. Mr. Nakasono was the one who suggested they think of it as time off, rather than an end to the job, but although they said it would be for a month, it was the last time he would see Momoko in her apron.

My uncle tried to think of all the little things that might make Momoko happy. He even tried to get her to go on a trip before she began her stay at the hospital. But what Momoko wanted was to relax at home.

My uncle suspected she was worried about him, since she knew how reluctant he was to take time off from the bookshop. "One trip is enough," she told him firmly. "Take care of the shop. I could watch you look after the shop all day long." After he'd heard that, my uncle didn't bring it up anymore.

It was around that time that everyone they knew in Jimbocho learned of Momoko's condition. Like me, when they first heard the news, they couldn't really believe it. "Not our Momoko?" People like Sabu pressed for more information—he even called me on the phone and demanded almost angrily that I give more details. And yet, in accordance with Momoko's wishes that we keep things the same, no one acted as if they were particularly worried for her, not on the surface at least, and no one showed her how heavy-hearted they were.

Until she was hospitalized, Momoko had more free time because she was off from her job at the restaurant, so she often dropped by the Saveur. At times, she would get into conversations with Sabu, the owner, and even Takano. Momoko was cheerful there too, and she was even relaxed enough to tease Sabu and the others about being so dispirited. And she adored the milkshakes the owner made for her, and always seemed happy whenever she had one.

Once the two of us had tea with Wada. That was when Momoko deliberately came out and said, "How's Wada #2 these days?" She seemed delighted with the result, and sat back and watched as Wada very earnestly asked, "Wada #2? Who is that? Am I Wada #1 then?"

Then as if she were remembering something, Momoko turned to Wada and said suddenly, "Look after Takako, will you? She can be indecisive, but she's a good kid." It didn't sound like Momoko at all.

I was taken aback, and I sat there wide-eyed with surprise as Wada, sitting next to me, answered, "Of course."

Around this time, my uncle always seemed depressed. He somehow seemed to be feeling much worse than Momoko. Even still, he ran the bookshop as usual, and now and then I went by to see how he was doing.

"Uncle, are you okay?" I would ask, feeling worried.

He would always answer, "Oh, I'm fine."

But he didn't look the least bit fine.

If I said anything more, he would get annoyed and take offense, so instead, I brought up a topic that I thought might make him feel better.

"You don't have any books to recommend, do you?"

"Hmmm? Oh, that's right. I can't think of anything now, but I'll find something for you next time."

Even when it came to a subject he normally would've jumped at the chance to talk about, he could only muster this listless response. And then of course he started sighing again.

"Um, is there anything at all I can do?" It was a sincere offer. Seeing the sullen look on my uncle's face was more than I could bear.

If there was a way I could be of help, I wanted to do it no matter what it was. But my uncle looked back at me astonished, as if to say, *What are you talking about?* "You've already done so much for us. You even accompanied her when she went to the hospital. I can't ask you to do any more than you've already done. It's too much," he said. Then he gave a weak laugh and that was all.

In that moment the Morisaki Bookshop, which used to resound with the sound of my uncle's cheerful voice, now seemed a terribly desolate place.

In the beginning of February, a week after Momoko had been admitted to the hospital, the doctor declared she had six months left to live. But even after my uncle told me this, it still didn't feel real to me at all. They were just meaningless words. I found it impossible to imagine that within that time frame Momoko would be gone. More than anything, I couldn't detect the slightest indication of it from Momoko, who was breathing and smiling at this very moment.

Death itself seemed far off in the distant future. This was Momoko—couldn't she just laugh it off and make it go away altogether? It seemed just about possible when you looked at her.

When I went to see Momoko at the hospital it was mostly to confirm this. When I saw that she looked exactly the same, secretly it would ease my mind. I really said to myself, "Oh, doesn't she look fine, she must be healthy. In October, or even September—once it's cool outside, we should go to Mount Mitake again together."

One day later that month, when Momoko was lost in her knitting as usual, I asked her to go with me. The two of us could climb the mountain on the funicular like we did last time and stay at that same mountain inn that was basically a hostel. Haru and the innkeeper must still be there now. Let's go see them again. Then we could look out from the viewing platform at the mountains stretching across that gorgeous landscape, and at night we could put our futons together and sleep side by side.

"It's a good idea, isn't it? You said yourself that you had a good time," I said, now at the edge of my chair.

"Yeah . . ." Momoko hunched her shoulders as if the whole idea seemed like too much of a hassle. "But Takako, you just complained the whole time that you were tired and your feet hurt."

"I'm not complaining now."

"You *were* complaining."

"I might have complained a little bit, but what if I say I won't complain this time?"

"Doubtful. You'll start whining right away."

"I'll make a vow not to, okay?"

"That reminds me, Takako. Remember when you fell down on the mountain right smack on your butt? That was brilliant," Momoko said with a mischievous grin.

Ultimately, the conversation came to an end without her offering a definitive answer about where she would or wouldn't go.

I could see in the courtyard on the other side of the hospital window that early cherry blossoms had already started to fall. Their petals spun in little whirls, dancing at the edge of the path.

14

Even after spring turned to summer, Momoko seemed as healthy as ever. I worried her condition might deteriorate in the intense summer heat, but her appetite was unchanged; even her complexion was good. She was in and out of the hospital for a while, but she even dropped by the Morisaki Bookshop, though she had to pause now and then to rest. One night when Tomo came to visit, the three of us went out to eat at Mr. Nakasono's place.

Yet, at the beginning of fall, when we would finally get a cool breeze in the afternoons, her condition took a turn for the worse. Momoko collapsed while she was recuperating at home. Her week of convalescence at home was canceled, and they quickly decided she needed to return to the hospital that day.

"It's time to prepare for the end. That's what the doctors told us yesterday," my uncle told me in a stiff voice over the phone. "Takako, when you have time, could you go see her again?"

This brief phone call from my uncle was all it took to obliterate the fleeting hope I'd held on to for half a year. And it was also in that instant when things finally became clear, the parts I'd been trying not to shine a light on, the reality I'd been trying desperately to turn away from.

The next day, I used one of my vacation days at work and rushed over to Momoko's room at the hospital. The anxiety and worry were tearing me apart as I opened the door to her room.

"Oh, Takako." I was struck by the sound of her voice. "You're back again?" It was the same speech she always gave. But there was no comparison between her voice then and how feeble she sounded now. There was no strength in her voice. Until then, I had rarely seen her lying down in bed, but today, perhaps because she was in pain, she didn't get up even when I came into the room. And only a week ago she'd seemed so healthy.

When her eyes met mine, she let out a laugh, almost like a shy little girl.

"Momoko . . ." Without meaning to, I said her name like I was about to cry. But I immediately regained my composure and did my best to smile. "My uncle called. It gave me a scare."

"I look pretty awful, don't I?"

Her new room was a single. Momoko was alone, lying in the middle of a white bed. The room was relatively large, but its size made it feel strangely oppressive. A great number of people had spent time in this room, in this very bed, and now they were gone. Somehow you could feel that keenly just by being in the room.

"Uncle Satoru?"

"He went back to the house a bit ago to change. It was so sudden we didn't have anything prepared."

"Oh . . ."

I waited there until my uncle returned. Unlike before, Momoko didn't try to hurry me and tell me to go home early. She lay there quietly.

When I was leaving, she muttered, "Takako, thank you for always coming to see me. Will you come back?"

"That doesn't sound like you, Momoko."

"I mean, it's embarrassing, don't you think? I only talk this way when I'm feeling weak."

"Sincerity is more becoming."

"Hey, you're talking to an old lady, you know."

"I'll come back soon. So, get some rest. Okay?"

Momoko turned just her head toward me, smiled, and said "Yes" meekly. I felt a warm lump inside. It was somewhere in my chest, throbbing. I could feel it rising inside me, like it was trying to find a way out. I left the room and leaned against the wall in the hallway. I looked up and stared into the fluorescent lights on the ceiling until the feeling passed.

From that point on, because my uncle often went to be with my aunt at the hospital, the Morisaki Bookshop was closed more frequently. Momoko objected, but no matter what she said to him, my uncle stubbornly refused to stop coming to the hospital.

I could see my uncle was getting skinnier. He was skinny to begin with, but he was far beyond that now; his body was shrinking so much that it was painful to look at him. Dark circles formed under his eyes, and his cheeks sank in; he seemed to age five years over the course of a few months.

He was always absent-minded—even to the point that at times a customer would be holding out a book in front of him, and he wouldn't notice.

"Uncle, you've got a customer," I'd say, gently nudging his shoulder.

"Oh, forgive me. I'm sorry," he'd say as he hastily accepted the book and rang it up. Once he was finished, however, he'd go back to staring off into space again.

There was no change in the shop's appearance. The books were put on the shelves where they belonged following my uncle's system of classification, and the place was scrupulously clean. Yet I couldn't help feeling that the shop now felt suffocating to be in.

I tried to tell my uncle gently that he might try to take a little break. But he wouldn't listen. "If I'm working," he told me, "I don't have to think about everything."

"But if you keep this up, you'll collapse."

"I'm fine. I'm not that fragile."

Even though he was normally so fragile that he was always whining, right now he was pretending to be tough.

"You know Momoko was trying to apologize for everything she put me through. Hearing her actually say it aloud threw me off. I didn't know how to respond. That's why I have to prove to her that I'm doing just fine."

"Uncle . . ." I couldn't find the words to say.

"I'm useless," my uncle mumbled to himself. He was sitting astride Roy, still staring off into space, lost in grief. "The past six months, I wanted to resign myself to letting her go, but it's no use. As the moment gets closer, I just want to be with her for as long as I can. I keep selfishly wishing for her not to die yet. She's already resigned herself to it. In the end, I'm the one who can't accept it. I'm just being greedy."

"You're not greedy," I said firmly.

My uncle shook his head.

"No, I am. Lately I find myself thinking that I'd sacrifice anything if it meant she would live even a little bit longer." My uncle smiled grimly. "I'm hopelessly selfish," he added in conclusion, and then he suddenly seemed to come back to himself, and he looked at me.

"I'm sorry. I'm just complaining."

"It's okay. The only thing I can do to help is to listen."

It really was about the only thing I could do. It broke my heart to be so powerless.

My uncle, ignoring how despondent I was, suddenly shouted "Oh" and stood up. "It smells like sweet olive blossoms," he said, and inhaled deeply and closed his eyes.

I took a breath too, caught up in the excitement.

"I guess it's already that time of year," I said.

My uncle gave his first proper smile of the day.

"Momoko's always liked this scent. I hope she can smell it at the hospital too." My uncle closed his eyes for a long time, like he was making a wish.

The days went by, and time kept on passing. No one can stop that.

The last time I saw Momoko was a quiet afternoon in the beginning of October. The autumn air blowing in through the open window felt pleasant, and the scent of sweet olive blossoms was carried into the room. The curtains swayed slightly in the breeze. Surrounded by this quiet, you could hear the soft sound of rustling fabric. That's the kind of afternoon it was.

When he saw me come in, my uncle mumbled something about having an errand to run and quickly left the room. Looking back, I think it was probably his thoughtful way of giving us some time alone, since he knew it might be the last time Momoko and I saw each other.

"Hey, can I talk to you about something?" Momoko said, once she opened her eyes after nodding off for a while. "I feel much better today. And I'm in the mood for a story."

"What kind of story?"

"Any kind. How about a memory from when you were a kid?"

Caught short by the sudden request, I thought through what kind of memory might fit the situation. A funny story would be good. Something to make her laugh. Something to let her forget about the pain she was in, even if only for a moment.

"Now that you mention it, there was this one time that my uncle took me to a summer festival. It was before you two got married."

"Really? Satoru did this?"

"It was the last night of our usual summer trip to my grandfather's house. In the distance, we could hear the music from the festival in their neighborhood. I was whining because I wanted to go so badly. My mother said we had a flight the next morning so we should go to bed early, but I loved being with my uncle, and the thought that we wouldn't be there the next day made me miss him so much. And so he brought me to the festival. My uncle was in high spirits too, of course. Ultimately, the festival ended right after we arrived, but I was content that I got to go. It was this incredible feeling, like I'd won something. We couldn't buy anything at the stalls, so my uncle bought us ice cream at a convenience store nearby, and the two of us walked back together, eating our ice cream and feeling sad."

As I talked, I could vaguely recall the light of the paper lanterns, the sound of the crowds of people talking, and even the way the afternoon heat lingered in the evening air. I'd forgotten about that, but now it felt like a really precious memory.

"That's all. I'm sorry. I wish I'd thought of a more interesting story."

Momoko was gazing up at the ceiling as I apologized. She slowly shook her head. "I can imagine it somehow. That scene . . . It's wonderful. I wish I'd been there. I wish I'd gone to a festival with Satoru and you when you were a child."

"No way, Momoko. I told you we barely even made it there."

"But isn't that just so like the two of you?" Momoko said and giggled, and I ended up laughing too. At least I meant to laugh, but then I felt something cold drip on the back of my hand. Before I had time to react, it was like raindrops were falling from my face onto my hands. No, I can't, I thought, but it was already too late.

I had decided I wasn't going to cry in front of Momoko. I thought it would be shameful, since she was the one suffering the most. Although I'd decided I wouldn't cry, on that afternoon alone it was no use. Once I let go, there was no stopping it. That lump that had been growing inside my chest had found a way out.

"I'm sorry," I apologized as I tried to find a way to stop my tears. But once those emotions had found an outlet, there was no reasoning with it, the tears kept coming and coming.

"I'm sorry. I'm so sorry." I hung my head, repeating the same words over and over, and Momoko reached out her hand and touched my hair, and stroked my head like she was taking it in her arms.

"It's okay," she said, almost whispering in my ear. "Don't apologize."

Hearing Momoko whisper gently to me like that made me cry even more.

"But . . . I am sorry."

"Takako, don't apologize, okay?"

I managed to nod through my tears. Momoko weakly pinched my cheek. Her fingertips were very cold. On impulse, I took her pale, cold hand in mine and held it tight. Such a small hand. Momoko had always had small hands, like a little girl. But now they felt so much smaller. As soon as I held her hand, it seemed to shrink, and it seemed like it might go on shrinking until it vanished like a dusting of snow.

"Thank you for crying over me," Momoko said. "When you're sad, don't try to hold it in. It's okay to cry a lot. The tears are there because you've got to go on living. You're going on living, which means there'll be more things to cry about. They'll come at you from all sides. So don't ever try to hide from the sadness. When it comes, cry it out. It's better to keep moving forward with that sadness; that's what it means to live."

Yes, I nodded, holding her hand tightly in mine. The scent of the sweet olive blossoms lingered faintly in the room. Even as I went on sobbing, I could smell it.

"Hey, Takako, I don't regret anything. I think I was really lucky that I got to see Satoru again, and I got to spend the time I had left with him at my side, and I was given the time to say goodbye.

What's more, I even got to become close with you. I couldn't wish for any more than that."

So that was it. Momoko had come back to my uncle because she wanted to say goodbye. Maybe the reason why she didn't seem any different after she found out about her relapse was that her wish had already come true. And even after she was hospitalized, and she lived under the watchful eye of the people around her, she always seemed dignified. Because she truly had no regrets.

After she told me this, she went on talking. "But, um . . . there's just one thing I still worry about after I die," she said abruptly. "I feel bad asking you this because I've already imposed on you so much, but I do have one final request. Can I ask you one more thing?"

"A request?" I looked at her, with my nose running and my face wet with tears. She stared back at me intently, her eyes full of determination.

"You know Satoru hasn't once let me see him grieving since he learned my cancer had relapsed. He smiles, and I can see in his face that he's always carrying the whole burden himself. But I'm painfully aware how sad it makes him to see me like this. He denies it, of course. But my worry is that after I'm gone, he won't let himself cry, and he won't let himself be dependent on anyone, and that he'll live trying to bear the burden of this grief himself. Because he's a very kind and a very foolish man."

"I see."

In the back of my mind, I pictured my uncle's pained smile, and it made my heart break.

"That's why if it seems like Satoru isn't able to cry after I die, I want you to be with him. We never had any children, so you're the only person I can think of to ask. If Satoru closes himself off from the world, yell at him and make him cry. What I hope more than anything is that if he cries, he'll be able to move forward."

Momoko squeezed my hand hard. Her face contorted like she was in pain.

"I'm sorry. It's selfish of me to ask this of you."

I looked Momoko in the eye and said, "I'll do it. I promise." I wanted her to know that I'd understood.

"Thank you. That's a huge relief," she said, and the look on her face finally softened into a smile. It was a tender smile that showed how deeply relieved she felt now. Then she gently wiped the tears from my face with her handkerchief. Like a child with its mother, I closed my eyes and didn't move a muscle as she wiped all my tears away. We stayed that way for a long time.

It was a truly peaceful afternoon. The cream-colored curtains swayed quietly in the breeze.

Momoko died in the early morning, three days later.

15

The funeral was held at my uncle's house. It was a bright and sunny October day, worthy of Momoko. Momoko's parents had passed away when she was young, and the few relatives in attendance were people like my parents, but instead, there were many people she knew from Jimbocho: Sabu and the other bookshop regulars, then the owner of the Saveur and Takano, Mr. Nakasono and the familiar faces from the restaurant, plus the innkeeper and the people she'd worked with at the mountain inn . . . and of course, Wada and Tomo. Tomo and the innkeeper rushed over right away to assist with the preparations for the wake, and they were a tremendous help when my mother and I found ourselves shorthanded.

From that alone, I could see how much everyone loved Momoko, how precious she was, and it made me profoundly happy. And everyone was in agreement that it should be a cheerful sendoff. Right up to the end, Momoko had kept smiling her reassuring smile, as radiant as a flower in bloom. Clearly, it would've been wrong to say goodbye to a person like that with a grim funeral.

As we gathered around her coffin at the wake, we laughed together like we always did. Sabu, who was quite drunk, launched into an endless monologue that lasted more than thirty minutes about how he wasn't able to fulfill his promise to Momoko to share one of his talents with her: performing some traditional *naniwabushi* ballads for her. In the end, his wife actually told him not to embarrass himself. A woman, who was Momoko's distant relative, scowled at us as if to say there was something inappropriate in us carrying on like this, but she completely misread the situation. There was sadness in it too. We just wanted to express our grief in a way that would make Momoko happy.

It was a good funeral, I think, one that will remain with us. I'm still convinced that it made Momoko happy. Momoko seemed at peace in her coffin, even cheerful. We talked about it. "Momoko looks good," we said; "she kind of looks like she's enjoying this along with us"; "definitely."

Yet there was one thing that worried me.

It was Uncle Satoru. He hardly opened his mouth during the funeral. He didn't touch any of the food or drink. All he did was go around bowing politely to everyone who'd come, expressing his gratitude again and again. Even when Momoko was cremated, he just gazed up at the sky while Sabu and the owner of the Saveur wiped away their tears. He had such a distant look in his eye, it was like he was trying to see to the outer limits of Earth's atmosphere. If he had broken down and cried at that moment, we were prepared to warmly welcome him into the fold. To be honest, I hoped he would. I hoped he would let himself depend on us. To mourn with us, and, if possible, to allow us to offer some words of comfort. But my uncle wouldn't show any weakness in front of others.

My uncle was the one who was with Momoko at her deathbed. I don't know what it was like. I don't know what he thought or what he said at that moment. Yet, based on how he was at the funeral, I got the impression that he was avoiding showing what he was feeling, just as Momoko had feared.

"*I think I'm* going to close the store for a little while."

It wasn't long after the funeral that my uncle made his announcement. I had stopped by the Morisaki Bookshop on my way home from work because I was worried about him. But the shutters were closed, even though it was still business hours. I got worried, and called my uncle at home right away; I had to wait awhile before he finally answered. When I asked him about it, he said, "I've decided to close for a while," sounding terribly exhausted.

I felt confused, and at the same time, a part of me thought, "Yes, of course." I'd had a slight hunch that he might say something like that soon.

"Are you in physical pain?" I asked.

"No, it's not that," he said, sounding listless on the other end of the line.

"Are you eating properly? Could I come over and make something for you?"

"I'm fine. I'm just a little tired. So . . ."

And with that the line went dead.

But my uncle had wasted away so much in the space of a month that I agreed that he should rest for a while. Get some proper rest, I thought, and when you're feeling better, come back to the shop. My uncle had already decided it was better that way.

I thought it would last a few days, certainly no longer than a week. Yet no matter how long I waited, the shutters of the Morisaki Bookshop remained closed. At some point, a handwritten sign on a piece of white paper had been stuck to the shutter, announcing, "We're closed for a while." The paper now dangled, after being battered by the wind and rain.

"How long is Satoru planning to wait till he opens the shop?" Sabu, who once seemed to come by every day, now seemed sad to have lost his place to go.

"I understand the feeling, but I still want Satoru to open the shop. We might not be much, but as regular customers, we can support him. But if he isn't around, then there's no way we can cheer him up."

On the phone, Sabu asked me to pass on the message when I saw my uncle.

He was right. There were other people who were waiting for the shop to open. But I would think my uncle already knew that . . .

The shop was still shuttered, and my uncle had let it remain closed for roughly a month. What was he doing all this time? He had basically shut himself up inside the house. Until Momoko passed away, he had insisted on running the shop, no matter what happened. Maybe he had put himself under too much strain, and now all at once it had come undone.

I went to the house in Kunitachi to see how he was doing. On the phone, he always told me he was eating right, but his voice sounded so listless that I decided to buy some groceries at the supermarket on the way so I could get him to eat something.

I stopped at a big supermarket near the train station that I'd been to many times with Momoko. She had a deep love for the place, because when they had sales the prices were much cheaper than the other stores nearby. It used to make me laugh when we went there together to see the way she would put the whole weight of her small, nimble frame on the shopping cart and then go gliding swiftly down the aisle. It was trivial little memories like this that kept coming back to me after she died. In those moments, it felt like I had a gaping hole in my heart. That's what it was like losing someone precious to you. I felt it now in so many different places and in so many different ways.

After I finished shopping, I headed for my uncle's house, walking down the alley of their residential street with supermarket shopping bags in both hands. Some dragonflies were flying across the sky, which was now bright red at sunset. One of them came down to me and acted as if it might land on my shoulder, then it flew off into the sky. As I walked, I felt like I was going to cry. I walked faster until I was moving at a brisk pace, rushing to get to my uncle's house.

Although I had told him I was coming that evening, he didn't answer the door when I rang the bell. It wasn't locked. When I let myself in and called to him upstairs, the only response I got was a "Yes" coming from my uncle's room.

Before I went up, I placed my hands together in prayer in front of the Buddhist altar to Momoko in the living room. The photograph on the altar had been taken six months earlier by a regular customer who was an amateur photographer. She was smiling, with the Morisaki Bookshop in the background. It was a wonderful picture. Seeing it brought back so many emotions.

Then I climbed up the stairs, knocked on my uncle's door, and opened it. Although the sun had already begun to set, my uncle was still in a sweatshirt and sweatpants, lying down on his futon. His hair was a mess, and he was so unshaven he looked like a cartoon burglar. He was in such a pitiful state that I blurted out, "Uncle!"

He looked at me drowsily and dumbly greeted me with a "Hey."

Was this how he'd been spending the whole day? There were bags of potato chips and bento containers from the convenience store scattered around the room.

"What are you doing?"

"Sleeping."

From an opening in the covers, my uncle thrust out both of his hands, flashing a peace sign.

"This is hardly peace!" I yanked off the covers, and my uncle curled up in a ball like a roly-poly bug. Undaunted, I threw open the curtains he'd drawn closed.

"Stop! If I'm exposed to light, I'll turn to ash."

"You idiot." I realized my voice sounded like I was about to cry. Why did I feel such relief? My uncle was still perfectly alive, he was still here. It's not that I actually believed that he'd end up following Momoko to the grave. But the way he'd been carrying the burden on his own lately made it seem like that wasn't out of the realm of possibility. Which is why it made me happy to see him there—even if he was acting like a roly-poly.

"Sorry, Takako."

"It's fine. What matters now is I'm making you dinner. Want to eat together? I'm sure you haven't had a proper meal in a while."

"Hey, thanks." He nodded obediently.

I took over the kitchen and made his favorite curry. Naturally, it was the Vermont Curry brand—mild. The kitchen didn't seem to have been used in a while. It was exceedingly clean.

I brought some egg drop soup and a plate piled with curry and salad into the living room and then I called out to my uncle. When I suggested he go wash his face and shave before eating, he obediently headed to the bathroom. I told him he ought to change his sweatsuit too because it was looking a little dingy, and he went up to the second floor and changed into another sweatsuit that was exactly the same color and style.

However, when I came into the living room and saw my uncle, I screamed. The area around his mouth was so covered in blood it was bright red.

"Huh, what?" My uncle's mouth hung open. He tried to approach me, and I shrieked.

"Blood! Blood!"

"Ah, I hadn't shaved in so long, I might've hacked myself up a bit," he said in a daze. He wiped his mouth with a tissue, but when he saw how stained with blood it was, he cried out, "Whoa, that's not looking good."

"Don't stand there 'whoa'ing. Try looking at yourself in the mirror."

"Why would I want to see how terrible I look?"

He was more or less aware, it seemed, of how terrible he looked. But even in moments like this he acted in a way that was hard to gauge, so I stayed vigilant.

Eventually, the two of us sat down at the table. His eyes still looked drowsy, and his expression was still the same as he shoveled the curry into his mouth robotically. It didn't feel like we were really having a meal together. Still, it was better than him not eating at all.

"Sabu and the others, they're worried about you. They want to see you back running the shop again." I passed on the message from Sabu, as I ate the curry that wasn't spicy enough for me.

"Oh, really? I feel bad about that."

"Everyone's waiting for you."

"Oh."

"How about we go together next time? I'll help you."

"I'll think about it."

There was no emotion behind what he was saying. He was just stringing words together. Then he said, "Sorry, I'm full," and put down his spoon. He hadn't even eaten half of it. He was still fairly weak. There was no way I could leave him like this. I had made a promise to Momoko, a promise that I would help him move forward and go on living. But I had absolutely no idea how to go about doing that. All I was able to do was make him meals, do some laundry, and be there for him to talk to. If he would at least open the shop, then I could be of more help to him.

I worried about this, and then I cautiously brought up the subject. "Uncle?"

"Yeah?"

"You aren't thinking about just leaving the shop closed like this, right? It's important to take some time off, of course. You're just taking some time off though, right?"

My uncle looked up as if what I'd said surprised him. But the gloomy look in his eyes returned and he looked down again.

"I don't know . . ."

"Uncle . . ."

"I genuinely don't know. It's not that I don't want to keep the shop. I am perfectly aware that our customers are waiting for me. It's just really hard. Momoko and I started at the bookshop together. Even when Momoko was gone, I ran the shop because I knew she was alive, even if she was living in a faraway place. Because I wanted to hold on to somewhere she could come back to, if she got tired or hurt, no matter what happened."

As he talked, my uncle's expression stiffened again. At times, his face contorted in pain.

"But it's really hard to be there right now. There are too many memories. And all those memories are vivid reminders that she's dead. I don't want the time to pass. Because if time passes, Momoko will drift further away from me."

My uncle stared at the clock on the wall across from me like he was giving it a glare.

The clock had been in use since my grandfather's era, and it was ticking away, still keeping time today. My uncle seemed to think he could stop the hands of that clock.

"I understand how you feel. At least, I think I do a little. I mean, I loved Momoko too. But you're making a mistake. You know it's a mistake, right? We're alive. There's no stopping time. So we have to keep on moving forward, one step at a time, no matter how heavy our legs feel." I felt a lump in my throat, but I kept on talking. "Even if it means leaving behind the person who died."

"Takako . . ."

I tried to look him in the eye as I talked, but he quickly looked away. I went on talking nevertheless. "You don't understand, Uncle. You taught me so many things. All the things you said. That's why even though it might not be clear in my head, I'm trying to find the words to get through to you. It's what you taught me, isn't it? How important it is to talk face-to-face and say what you have to say."

His eyes remained downcast the whole time, so it was hard to tell if he was listening. But in the end, he muttered a few words. He sounded like he'd given up. "You're right. I don't understand. But that's okay."

The Morisaki Bookshop remained closed after that too. The only thing I could think to do was keep the shop clean. If you leave old books shut in a room without air circulation, they'll mildew and become unsellable. I wanted to prepare the shop for when my uncle felt ready to reopen. I knew that was what Momoko would've wanted.

On the way home from work, I used the key I still had from when I lived in the building, and went in through the back door of the bookshop. Because it had been left for a whole month, the air was heavy and stagnant. It was filled with the scent of damp mildew. In the darkness, I felt around with my hands and ferreted out the switch. When I flipped it on, the fluorescent lights flickered to life, and it was suddenly bright inside. When I sneezed from the dust, the sound filled the room.

First, I opened all the windows and aired out the room. Then I took time to sweep the floors with a broom, then diligently wiped down the bookshelves and the floors with a dust cloth. Under the overly bright white lights, the shop looked terribly empty, like some storeroom deep underground. Just being in that room, I felt sadness growing inside me till it was unbearable. Even Roy, the do-nut pillow, neglected by his owner for such a long time, somehow seemed lonely.

My heart ached to see that this place that my uncle loved so much, that mattered to so many people, had now been discarded as if it were no longer needed.

I went upstairs to the second floor and watered Momoko's potted plants on the windowsill with her watering can. Having gone so many days without water, all of them had shriveled and now looked down as if they were cowering. "Sorry guys," I murmured as I watered each one thoroughly.

It was after nine o'clock when I left the shop. The night air was dry, and the wind was so cold it seemed to pierce my skin. I winced. In the darkness, the air I exhaled looked so white it shocked me.

The world was trying to usher in winter.

One season would give way to the next. The loss of a single person couldn't change that. It should've been obvious, but it now felt like an outrage.

I turned to look back at the bookshop and whispered, "Don't worry. I'll be back." Then I walked away.

"Takako, you're doing the right thing." Wada was comforting me on the phone.

Lately, I'd been feeling down all the time. Though I knew it was wrong, I'd find myself depending on Wada.

"But what I said didn't get through to him. I'm at a loss . . ."

What could I really do to get my uncle to move forward with his life again the way Momoko had asked?

"There's only so much you can do. Your uncle lost the person who mattered most to him. Maybe I shouldn't say this, but if it were me, and I knew I would never see Momoko again, then I might give it all up too."

I found myself imagining the reverse scenario. I only imagined it for an instant, but it made everything go black in my mind. He was right; I was truly sad that Momoko was dead, but there was no way it could come close to the sadness my uncle felt. I regretted how I'd righteously told my uncle at his house that I understood how he felt a little bit. For my uncle, Momoko was what Kazue was for Sakunosuke Oda.

"For my uncle, I guess, the Morisaki Bookshop is also a symbol of all the time he spent with Momoko."

There are too many memories in the bookshop. I remembered what my uncle looked like as he said that to me. Memories that stretched across twenty years, of happiness and sorrow, had accumulated in that site, layer upon layer.

"He must find those memories unbearable right now," Wada said. "But the time will come when the place will be precious to him precisely because it holds all those memories. Until that day comes, maybe you just have to put your faith in him, and wait for him to be ready."

"That's all I can do now."

After that, every few days I made time to head over to the shop. All I did was air it out, clean, and check that there were no signs of mildew in the collection. But it was enough to make sure that he could open the shop anytime he was ready.

On one of those nights, Tomo accompanied me. To tell the truth, it was sometimes hard for me to be in the bookshop alone at night; I would find myself remembering all kinds of things. So, I was grateful that she was with me.

Working together, we finished cleaning in less than a half hour. Tomo was so full of enthusiasm she suggested we try to straighten up the collection of books on the second floor, but I dismissed the idea, telling her we'd do it some other time, because if we started now, we'd never make the last train.

I felt indebted to Tomo for coming, and for her help at Momoko's funeral. I was truly grateful. This seemed like a good moment to tell her again how thankful I was.

As usual, she was too modest. "No, no, please. It was nothing," she said.

"But you really have gone to so much trouble on my behalf," I said, insisting on telling her how grateful I was.

"When I go back at the end of the year, I think I'm going to see my sister's former boyfriend again," she said suddenly.

"What? Really?"

"I am. I'm going to apologize to him properly. He's been worried about me all this time, it seems, yet I've been avoiding him. It might sound like an exaggeration, but I feel I need to set things right. I think once I do, I'll be able to see a way forward."

"Oh, I think that's absolutely wonderful."

I was delighted to hear Tomo had come so far. I supported it wholeheartedly.

"It's thanks to you and Takano that I was able to get to this point."

"No, no," I said, flustered. "I really didn't do anything."

She giggled.

"Now you're the one saying that. We're just alike. I'm not here today because I want you to thank me. And the same goes for you. That's just how we are."

Then something happened at the beginning of December, around the time I noticed the neighborhood was lit up in glittering lights for Christmas.

On that night, I went again to the shop to air it out and clean up, following my usual routine. I had more or less finished my work, and had told myself it was time to go home, but I made no attempt to leave. For some reason, I found it hard to go. I thought, Let me stick around a little longer. For no particular reason, I sat down at the counter in my usual seat, staring off into the distance. Although I'd turned on the heat, I'd had the windows open until a few minutes earlier, so it was as cold inside the shop as it was outside. I rubbed my hands together and wondered how long it would take to warm up.

When I looked at the clock on the wall, it said it was nearly ten. I should leave soon, I thought, but my body wouldn't budge. Outside the window, a lively group went down the street, probably on their way home from an end-of-the-year party.

By chance, my gaze landed upon the account book tucked away in the utility cabinet below the counter. Though we called it an account book, there was nothing major written in it. It was the sort of thing where we wrote down the books we sold and the price. The leather-bound book my uncle normally used was thicker and threadbare from years of use. This one was thinner, and still relatively new. What's going on here? I thought, and pulled out the account book that had been pushed all the way in the back like someone was trying to hide it.

When I opened it up, I blurted out, "Oh . . ." On each page, there was something written in densely packed characters.

They were things that Momoko had written. It was not quite a diary, it was more like simple notes, but she recorded the date and the weather, along with things that went on in the bookshop. The dates began not long after Momoko suddenly returned home and started living on the second floor of the bookshop.

"Satoru, sold books again today, in a good mood."

"Setting aside the Ōgai Mori book Mr. Kurada wants."

"Don't forget to organize the book carts!"

"Sold nothing before noon because of the rain. Heartache."

"Takako isn't doing so well today? Worried."

After I read the first few pages, I closed the book suddenly. Some of Momoko's thoughts were still here in these pages. The days she spent with my uncle and me were inscribed in this book. It might not be a masterpiece to be read for generations, or a text left by a great writer, but for my uncle and me it was precious.

I needed my uncle to read it right away. With that thought in mind, I got up from my chair, but in that instant the back door was thrown open with a bang, and I jumped back in surprise. When I looked over, I saw that my uncle was somehow standing in the entrance, breathing heavily. And with a look of shock on his face. But his expression quickly changed to disappointment when he saw me.

"Oh, it's you, Takako," he muttered with a weak smile. "I found myself back in the neighborhood walking past the bookshops. Then I saw the lights were on in the shop . . ."

I didn't have to ask what happened next. I could tell just by looking at the expression on his face. My uncle tricked himself into believing Momoko was inside, despite the fact that there was no logical reason why that should be. I, on the other hand, was so stunned by my uncle's sudden appearance that I couldn't speak.

"Takako . . . ?" My uncle was staring at me with a baffled look on his face.

I couldn't shake the feeling that something strange was happening here, something I couldn't put into words. There must be some other power at work here. The timing was too much. First I find Momoko's writing in the account book, and then at the very moment when I wish I could show it to my uncle, he comes bursting into the room . . .

"So, um," I said, still feeling overwhelmed. I stood in front of my uncle and held out the account book. "This is the account book Momoko wrote in."

"Momoko?" For a moment, my uncle just stared blankly at the book in my hands, then he slowly reached out his hands to take it.

"Maybe I should sit down?"

My uncle sat on Roy, and gently turned the pages of the account book. As he carefully read through each handwritten line, he suddenly cracked a smile. "When did she start doing this?"

"I know, right?"

Finally the heater was kicking in, and the room began to warm up. My uncle turned the pages, as if transfixed. I could hear the rustling of paper. I thought I might make tea, but right when I went up to the second floor to get the teapot and teacups, I heard my uncle suddenly shout, "Ah!"

"What is it?" I peeked suspiciously over his shoulder, then I called out too. There on the last page of the book was a long passage that began "To Satoru . . ." She had noted the date too: it was two days before she collapsed and had to be taken to the hospital in an ambulance.

"It's . . ." I said, and my uncle nodded silently without looking away from the book. His hand was trembling slightly.

"Uh, maybe I should step outside for a bit?"

"No, it's okay. Stay here."

"Got it," I said, and then I stayed quiet.

After my uncle had taken some time to read through what she'd written, he gazed up at the ceiling for a long while. Then he stood up straight and read through it slowly once more. During that time, I walked up and down the aisles, looking around the shop restlessly. I was caught off guard when my uncle suddenly tried to hand me the account book without saying a word.

"That's okay. I don't need to read it," I said.

"It's fine. I want you to." He was looking right at me, holding out the book as if urging me to hurry up and take it.

I hesitated for a moment, but eventually I took the book.

To Satoru,

How long will it take for you to find this? If you've already gotten back on your feet again, then there's really no need to read this. In that case, feel free to blow your nose in it and toss it in the trash.

I thought about leaving a will, but then I'm sure you would've read it right away. That seemed pointless, so I decided instead to leave this for you. So, please read it as an alternative to a will.

Unfortunately, I didn't end up outliving you. I guess this is my fate somehow. I apologize that I had to be the one to leave first.

It breaks my heart to leave you behind because you're such a crybaby. Even when you proposed to me, you cried. "You might be fine without me," you said, "but I'd be useless without you." At the time, I laughed and said, "This guy's a mess," but I was really happy. There's no one else on earth who could have told me something so pathetic and wonderful. After all, I would be useless without you too.

Afterward, through the joy and sorrow, we had many happy times together. But I know I caused you a lot of trouble. Still, you took me in after I chose to leave. And you asked me to come back. You're so infuriatingly kind. So kind that you wouldn't let me go in the end. You never gave up on me.

I've decided that from now until the day I die, I'm going to say "thank you" to you every day without fail. It still won't be enough to express my gratitude for all that you've done for me, but I'd be happy if I can show at least a small portion of how much I owe you.

Um . . . my writing is getting more and more discombobulated. Is that how you write discombobulated? If I'm wrong, please don't snap at me, okay?

Anyhow, here's my request: just as I have wonderful memories of being with you, I don't want you to let your memories of me be sad, I want you to remember the fun and happiness. If you find yourself spending every day in the same anguish you felt when I was in the hospital, you've got to know that's not what I hoped for. I want you to smile. I love the way you smile.

There are a lot of people around you who will support you. Remember that, and lean on them. There's one particular person I trust and love above all, and I'm going to ask her to do a little something for me.

One more thing.

Please give my regards to the Morisaki Bookshop. The proof that we were together lies there. I know how much you love the shop, and the truth is I love it too. If I'd been able, I would've wanted to see you working there just a little bit longer. After all, it's when you're in the shop that you shine the brightest. Of course, it was just a selfish wish on my part. But if that's the case, I hope that after this you and the Morisaki Bookshop can move forward together.

Please look after the shop. It's full of our memories together, and the memories of so many other people too.

Momoko Morisaki

She never played fair, did she? If she had this up her sleeve, she could have at least told me. Did she anticipate that my uncle would close the shop? Or had she left it as some kind of insurance? I didn't know, but what I did know was that this note was full of love for my uncle and the Morisaki Bookshop. And this shop was teeming with the thoughts and hopes and feelings she experienced in her life.

And she referred to me as the person she "trusted and loved above all."

"She really was such a troublemaker." When I handed back the account book, my uncle gave me a bitter smile. "Takako, what did she ask you to do? Was it too much trouble?"

"That doesn't matter now, Uncle," I said and my uncle looked back at me, his eyes wide with surprise.

"What?" he said, and smiled at me.

"Momoko told me, 'I want him to fully grieve, and then look ahead and go on living.'"

"No, Takako, I . . ."

But I went on, ignoring my uncle's attempt to respond. "I can't really do anything for you. I can't do anything but cry with you. So, you don't have to grieve alone anymore."

My uncle stared intently at the account book in his hand as if trying to resist it. He looked hard at it for a long time. And then just as I realized his lips were trembling slightly, he suddenly let out a scream that sounded like the call of some wild beast. He raised his voice as if straining to force out all the air inside him and channel it into a wordless scream. I went to his side and rubbed his back that now seemed so skinny. When I looked at my uncle, my eyes suddenly filled with tears.

"When I went to see her in the hospital, she always said 'Thank you.' I told her to stop because it was disconcerting, but she kept on . . . even at the end . . ."

Now both of us were openly sobbing. We wailed out loud and cried uncontrollably. My uncle crouched and covered his face like he was going to collapse right then and there. I stayed beside him and rubbed his back, ignoring the tears dripping from my face onto the floor.

Our sobs echoed in the bookshop late into the night. Our voices, reverberating inside the room, made the air tremble. It was as if the shop itself joined in to mourn Momoko's death with us. As if it too were grieving.

We went on crying for as long as we needed to.

No matter how much we cried, our tears would not run dry.

That sound will echo in the shop forever.

The night gently enveloped us, my uncle and me, and the whole Morisaki Bookshop.

Surprisingly, it was Wada who told me the following evening that the Morisaki Bookshop had reopened for business.

"I've got good news," he said on the phone, sounding unusually excited. "I finished work early today, so I went by the bookshops in Jimbocho. And then I saw, believe it or not, that the lights were on in the Morisaki Bookshop," he said, almost without stopping to breathe.

"Is that right?"

I was still at work, but as I stood in the hallway of my office, I let out a sigh of relief.

"Huh? You don't seem that happy? Did you already hear it from your uncle or Sabu?"

"No, I just knew it was going to be okay. Thank you, my prince, for your efforts."

After last night, my uncle completely changed, and by the next day he was already opening the shop—that was just like him. I, on the other hand, embarrassed myself by going to work with my face still puffy from weeping my eyes out.

"Oh really? Anyway, it's good news. I was so happy it was like it was happening to me. I got very excited. And even better, when I went in, your uncle brought out tea and said something like, 'Thanks for coming to the funeral.'"

"What? Really?"

"And then I told him I was writing a novel set at the bookshop, and he told me to let him read it when I was finished. He said, 'If it's bad, I'll tear it apart for you.'"

"Hold on there. That's going too far," I said in shock.

"No, I was happy. I was really happy. Whatever the case, it's really good news, Takako."

"It is."

What happened that night seemed like a dream. How I'd suddenly noticed the account book, and how my uncle had appeared right then . . .

Maybe it was all Momoko's doing. She was worried about my uncle being lost in grief . . . The idea briefly crossed my mind, then I decided not to think about it anymore. No matter how much I thought it over, I'd never know. What mattered was that the two of us were looking ahead and going on living. That's all.

"My prince, do you think I should go over after work?"

"Sure, though your uncle will be gone by then."

"Yeah, but still."

"Well, how about the Saveur?"

"Sure."

"Got it."

Outside the window, the sky was already pitch black. The nearly full moon, missing only the slightest sliver, gave off a dazzling light.

It's my day off from work, and I'm walking the same familiar street. It may be sunny, but it's still a cold February afternoon. The sky is a soft blue with pale clouds drifting by that look like they were painted with watercolors. I feel warm in the gloves Momoko gave me.

Today, there's a feeling of calm in the air again as I walk through the neighborhood of bookshops in Jimbocho. The people I pass on the street walk at a leisurely pace. I go down a street lined with low buildings and turn onto a side street. And then, just as I expected, I hear someone loudly calling my name.

"Takako!"

I quicken my pace out of embarrassment, and as soon as I get close to the source of the voice, I start to protest. "I told you already—please don't shout my name in the middle of the street!"

"Why though?"

"Haven't I told you it's embarrassing?"

But no matter how often I say it, my uncle will always cause trouble like this. Still, hearing his voice, a part of me feels a sense of security too. This is a place where I belong. A place where I'm welcomed. That's how it feels.

"How are you?" my uncle asks with a big smile on his face.

"I'm good."

"All right, then. Got cold, didn't it? Come on, I'll make us some hot tea."

"Okay."

The Morisaki Bookshop has remained open, keeping its usual hours, ever since the day my uncle reappeared at the shop. It's open for business every day, from morning till night, just like before.

When my uncle initially reopened the shop, he looked at me, on the verge of tears, and whined, "What am I going to do? I've had zero income because I've been closed for more than a month." But despite his griping, there was a bit of excitement around the shop for a while after it reopened. Having heard the rumors, the regulars—Sabu chief among them—started coming by one after another every day. Thanks to which, my uncle's first essential duty after reopening was bowing to each of them to apologize for closing the shop. They were obviously happy, and there wasn't an angry customer among them. My uncle seemed happy to be warmly welcomed back by his many regular customers. The look on his face told me there was no need to worry about him anymore. Of course, he is never going to get over Momoko's death. He'll never fully recover. Yet my uncle has decided to look ahead. He's decided to take in the sadness with everything else and keep moving forward.

There's been a little change too on my end of things. Wada and I are getting married soon. We've already introduced each other to our parents, and now we're looking for a new home. Actually, part of the reason I came to the shop today was to deliver that news. However, my uncle still seems hostile to Wada, and when I casually bring up his name, he suddenly launches into a solemn speech. "What's going to happen to the secondhand book business with the rise of electronic dictionaries and the downturn in the publishing industry?"

Good grief. This guy can bore you to death with this stuff. If Momoko were here, I'm 100 percent sure that's what she'd say. It feels like Momoko's sitting right here, drinking tea with us.

"Well, my uncle's just that kind of guy, isn't he?" As I turn to where Momoko should be and give her a wry smile, my uncle looks at me with his mouth wide open, and says, "Huh? What?"

"Nothing," I lie and smile. "Hey, do you remember when we went to the summer festival together?"

"The summer festival?"

"Yeah, when I was a kid. Didn't we go to one together?"

"Oh, yeah, I guess that's right. We could hear the music, and you just had to go see it."

"That's right. And we ate ice cream from a convenience store and went home."

"You're right. That's it. It was a sad night." He laughs a little, recalling what happened. "But what makes you suddenly think about it now?"

"When Momoko and I were talking at the hospital and she asked me to do something for her, we talked about that night."

"Oh really?"

"She said she wished she'd been there with us."

"Oh."

"I think about that day a lot."

"You do?"

"I do. That's all I wanted to say."

The two of us sip our tea at the same time. I think of the expression on Momoko's face in that moment. My uncle, for his part, seems to be remembering something too. A slight smile forms at the edges of his mouth.

The two of us share this quiet moment thinking of her, and then the door opens with a soft sound. When I turn to look, I say "Hmmm?" aloud in spite of myself. The face that appears in the opening of the sliding door belongs to our mysterious regular: the old man with the paper bag. It's been a long time since he's come in.

The old man carries a paper bag full of books; the look on his face as he comes inside is the same as ever, but I stare at him like I'm ready to devour him with my eyes. That's because the sweater he's wearing is not his usual ancient artifact. It might be the same ashen color, but the one he has on now is a fairly gaudy substitute with a great big deer head stitched into it. On top of that it's new and there's not a single frayed hole in it.

What's even more surprising is that when the old man has rummaged through the shelves and brought several books to the register, he turns to my uncle and starts talking to him. "What's this? You've got things in order again, huh?"

This guy has not once opened his mouth to speak in all this time, no matter what.

Even my uncle looks a little bit surprised.

"Thank you very much. We were closed for a brief period," he says apologetically, as he scratches the back of his head.

"I thought you went out of business," the old man says in a low voice as he fidgets. Without waiting for my uncle to respond, he takes his books, stuffs them into his bulging paper bag, and abruptly leaves the shop.

My uncle and I leave the shop too, as if lured outside by the old man, and stand side by side watching him walk away with unsteady steps.

Overjoyed by our unexpected customer, I say to my uncle, "He looked healthy, didn't he?"

The old man gets farther and farther away until he's finally out of sight. It's cold outside with a chilly breeze, but the little street is lit up in the afternoon light.

"Ah, that was nice."

"He must've come by when you were closed."

"Yeah, I feel bad about that."

"New sweater though, right?"

"It was new."

"It was gaudy though, right?"

"It was gaudy."

"You think he couldn't wear the old one anymore so he got himself a brand-new one?"

"Takako?"

"Sorry, I know. Don't pry, right?"

"Right." My uncle nodded forcefully. He went on talking as if he were admonishing himself. "This is a bookshop. We sell books." The look on his face was cheerful, a little proud.

A writer I like left behind a passage like this in one of his books: "People forget all kinds of things. They live by forgetting. Yet our thoughts endure, the way waves leave traces in the sand." Deep down, I hope that's true. It gives me great hope.

A plane crosses the sky in the distance, leaving behind it a freshly born cloud.

"Hey, Uncle, see that cloud behind the plane?" I pointed to the sky, and my uncle looked up and squinted at it.

The cloud kept growing longer, drawing a bright white line all the way across the pale blue sky.

Here in Tokyo's neighborhood of secondhand bookstores is our little bookshop. It's full of little stories. And it holds within its walls the thoughts and hopes and feelings of a great many people.

Translator's Note

In Satoshi Yagisawa's previous novel, *Days at the Morisaki Book-shop*, Takako finds the book that changes her life by simply closing her eyes and reaching out her hand to pick one at random from the stack of texts beside her futon. One of the joys of the sequel is that it's a novel about the pleasures of searching for books. The truth is, we do not always know why we find ourselves looking for a particular volume. Sometimes, like Sabu, we're returning to an author we remember fondly. Other times we see a title mentioned in another book, like this one, and we're drawn to it as a subtle recommendation. We scan the shelves of some secondhand book-shop for the poetry collection Takako suggests would be ideal to read before bed: Kōtarō Takamura's *The Chieko Poems* (which exists in multiple translations, but I'd recommend the Green Integer edition, translated by John G. Peters, and Kodansha's 1978 edition by Soichi Furuta, which includes reproductions of artwork by Chieko herself). Sometimes looking for one book, we end up finding another. Hyakken Uchida's *Train of Fools* has not yet been translated, but readers can find some of his darker, dreamlike short fiction in Rachel DiNitto's translation, *Realm of the Dead*, or his lighter essays in *The Columbia Anthology of Japanese Essays*, edited and translated by Steven D. Carter. Or they can come to him, like many, through the affectionate tribute Akira Kurosawa paid to his life in his final film, *Madadayo*.

No matter if we are browsing a bookstand in an airport or searching for a rare first edition, our motivation often remains mysterious. The books lie ahead of us; they seem to know things we do not. An old friend once told me how coming across Jun'ichirō Tanizaki's *In Praise of Shadows* in college changed the course of his life. Satoru puts the book in Takako's hands, and tries to get her to read it on the spot. For Takako, reading becomes a way to open herself up to the world, but for her friend Tomoko, literature is a consolation, and, at times, a retreat from the world. Perhaps that's one reason why many of the authors mentioned in this novel are associated with the literature of decadence and the Burai-ha (from Baudelaire to Dazai, Sakaguchi, and Oda). Near the books of fantasy and science fiction on Tomoko's shelves, Takako finds books by the Belgian writer Georges Rodenbach, whose novel *Bruges-la-Morte* has been translated by both Mike Mitchell and Will Stone with its images of the city restored. It has the death-haunted atmosphere of a nineteenth-century *Nadja* or even *Vertigo* (both Sebald's and Hitchcock's).

Later in the novel, Takako and Takano set out in search of a book that, strictly speaking, does not exist. *The Golden Dream* is a book within a book that itself seems to have been invented for this novel, but that doesn't mean we shouldn't go looking for it. Who knows what else we'll find?

We tend to think of reading as a solitary act, but the book you are reading has only found its way into your hands thanks to the ingenuity and diligence of many. I am grateful to Satoshi Yagisawa and to my editor, Sara Nelson, for entrusting me with these delightful novels, and to Setsuko and Simon Winchester, who introduced me to Sara. I'm indebted to my sister, Melissa Ozawa, and Bruno Navasky for their patient and invaluable feedback, and to my father, Yuichi Ozawa, and my friend Hiroko Tabuchi, who helped me along the way. The book was also aided at key moments by my agent, Andrea Blatt, of WME, and at every stage, by my wife, Nicole, who read every word and who always knows where to find the books I'm missing. This translation is dedicated to my sons, Emile and Ilias, who are just discovering the pleasures of reading.

DON'T MISS
SATOSHI YAGISAWA'S
INTERNATIONALLY BESTSELLING DEBUT

"A familiar romance about books and
bookstores, told with heart and humor."

—*Kirkus Reviews*

HARPER ● PERENNIAL

DISCOVER GREAT AUTHORS, EXCLUSIVE OFFERS,
AND MORE AT HC.COM.